Different

by

Michael Frederick

Novels by author:

White Shoulders

Ledges

Missouri Madness

Shy Ann

Summer of '02

Autumn Letters

Places

Blue River

The Paper Man

Dedicated to my loyal readers and librarians

September, 2009/1st printing/5,000 copies

Thanks, Tony, for your art.
Cover Design by Anthony Conrad

Sweet

Finally! August 13th! Every single morning for the past eighteen years held the same breakfast — fried eggs over easy, fried potatoes, sausage patties, and toast with orange juice and coffee. Always good, but still always the same. And as he had every morning, tall and lean Mickey Allen Ditwell tramped down the rickety stairs of the Ditwell farmhouse dressed in black jeans and a worn black T-shirt with black high-top Nikes. He saw the back of "Bert's" hulking frame standing at her kitchen stove putting two eggs, a full spatula of potatoes, one sausage patty, and two pieces of wedge-cut, homemade rye toast onto his plate. Mickey's special plate was a gray-blue porcelain plate he'd been using since he was in grade school.

Bert's husband, Ned Ditwell, had just finished swirling clean his plate with his last bite of burnt-black toast and was now ready to reach for a toothpick and pick up where he left off in his morning paper.

Ned and Bertha Ditwell were both seventy years old. Both were six-foot-two and built for work — long hours of work on their Madisonville, South Dakota, farm. Bert and Ned did the kind of work their only grandson wanted no part of. Many times over the years Mickey had to remind his grandparents of today. The day he turned eighteen was the day he was free.

Even though Mickey's eighteenth birthday had finally arrived, he received the same morning greeting. Bert with her back to him said "mornin'" above the diminishing sizzle made by her snapping lard in her giant, black, cast-iron frying pan. Then Ned, chewing his last bite of egg yolk and toast, groaned out "uh-huh" from behind his open *Dakota Falls News* without missing a word he was reading.

As he had every morning, Mickey entered the dining room on this long-awaited day. His eyes went to the plastic-framed, embroidered inscription on the wall above the breakfast table. "Having a place to go ... is home. Having someone to love ... is family. Having both ... is a blessing." And as he did every morning, he said his favorite word and his morning greeting. "Sweet." Depending on his mood, he would say it in a variation of tones. Sometimes he enunciated the Es in a high-pitched elongation, or else he uttered it in a mumbling groan when he was bored to tears — as he was most mornings.

Bert lit a single tiny candle and poked it into one of the birthday boy's wedge-shaped pieces of thick toast. While half-singing "Happy Birthday" without managing to properly hit a single note, she delivered her ungrateful grandson's steaming breakfast.

Ned lowered his newspaper, revealing his cataract-glossy blue eyes through his black-framed reading glasses he'd purchased five years ago at the Dakota Falls Wal-Mart with a twenty-percent-off coupon. He dipped his pointed chin and said, "Yep ... eighteen today." Then he courtesy-smiled without removing the toothpick planted at one corner of his thick, brooding, Germanic lips.

"Sweeeet!" Mickey responded, indicating he was in a good mood on this very special and long-awaited day — the one he thought would never get here.

Bert flashed Ned a knowing look that said, *Yeah, we know what eighteen means ... It means the end of those thousand-dollar monthly checks that Mickey's mother has been sending on time for eighteen years.* Mickey knew who really sent the money every month. It came from his father. A man he had never met. A man who was famous. A man who was about eighty years old and living in southwest Minnesota between two little towns. Mickey had found the place on a map that Ned kept in the glove box of his beige 1993 Buick Century, which was always kept in perfect running condition. Both the car and the map would play into Mickey's plans later in the month.

Today's mail was the most important part of Mickey's plan, but it wouldn't be delivered for two more long hours. It would bring his birthday check from his mother. On his last three birthdays she had sent three hundred dollars, but how much would come today — his eighteenth birthday? He couldn't wait to see what lay inside the card that he would toss away without hesitation. Because they were all signed "Love, Mom," Mickey always threw away the cards without even reading them.

Mickey had his mother's tall, lean frame and her brindle-colored hair. It was thick with lots of body, and he wore it in a short spike that stayed vertical all day without gel. He referred to his selfish, gold-digging mother as "Marilyn," except whenever she drove to the farm every three or four months in her rich boyfriend's new white Cadillac. She had gotten a new Cadillac every year since she moved in with the Cadman, a new-car dealer in Dakota Falls. Mickey would call her "mom" as little as possible, and he liked it when he didn't have to say it at all.

His anticipation of this special day had been the cause of his worst-ever acne flare-up. He'd been picking and squeezing his face in so many places that even his mouth at each corner had dried-blood scabs. But he kept picking and picking until it hurt every time he ate or opened his mouth to speak.

Mickey's carefully concocted plan to be free was nearing and had to be put into action before the end of the month. He was glad his uncaring grandparents would no longer be receiving the monthly support checks that were mailed to the farm — money sent by a man who never claimed his son.

As the new young adult sat eating his breakfast, he was worried about how to avoid having to live with his mother. Last Christmas she had taken him to lunch and given him a hundred bucks for Christmas. She knew her parents wanted her son off the farm as soon as the support checks ended, so she told Mickey he could live with her in the "Cadman's" nice house in Dakota Falls starting September 1st. That was the main reason Mickey's face looked so awful with festering whiteheads in a dozen places. He didn't want to live with his mother at all.

At Christmastime, she had driven her brooding son to the city in that big white Cadillac, and they had lunch at their usual upscale restaurant. For the past two years Marilyn talked about her colon cancer, which was in remission from her chemo treatments she'd been getting at a Dakota Falls clinic.

Never did Marilyn discuss her daughter, Katie. She was Mickey's fourteen-year-old half-sister who happened to live in the same town as Mickey's famous father, Wallis Pond. Of course, Katie had a different father whom she lived with ever since Marilyn left them to live with the Cadman over three years ago. Mickey had never met Katie or Karl Spink. He did, however, meet the Cadman once a year ago when the car dealer drove to Madisonville to pick up Marilyn's son at the farm.

Mickey Ditwell had never been confused about his dysfunctional family because that's how it had always been. Different.

Marilyn was Bert and Ned's only child and most certainly a handful. Attractive Marilyn Ditwell had run away from the farm not long after she turned seventeen. Her parents never had a good thing to say about their daughter, even though Marilyn had gone straight to work. She began her career at Wallis Pond just days after stepping off the bus from Madisonville.

Wallis Pond was a two-story commercial building half a block long and close to the Big Sioux River in downtown Dakota Falls. Wallis Pond Beauty College was the Midwest's largest and most prestigious beauty school. Wallis Pond instructors would train young stylists in every detail needed to run a full-service beauty salon. Every year, hundreds of young women like Marilyn would leave their rural communities in Iowa, Nebraska, North Dakota, South Dakota, and Minnesota to learn a trade that the man Wallis Pond knew as well as any man or woman involved in the art of hairstyling.

This five-state area in America's heartland Wallis called "Superland." Over dozens of years of traveling Superland's hundreds of towns by land and by air, the incredible Wallis Pond became wealthy beyond anyone's imagination — especially his own.

Wallis Pond's unclaimed son and only child — to his knowledge, anyway — stood on the rural gravel road near the mailbox smack-dab in the middle of his father's Superland. Mickey Allen Ditwell had inherited his father's prominent nose and dull gray eyes; however, the greatest inheritance he'd been given was between his ears in that mysterious place of gray matter where imagination lives.

In the distance, visible in the August haze of pollen, was the white Jeep that would deliver him from the place his parents had chosen for him. Now it would be his turn to call his own shots in a world gone mad with terrorism, economic fears, and a thousand uncertainties. As the Jeep closed in on the Ditwell mailbox, Mickey said just under his breath, "Sweeeet."

Forty-year-old, orange-haired Edward Lesley Dense had something his unremarkable parents could never give him: Consciousness. E. L. Dense used to be a writer. In over sixteen years he hadn't written a word. He had self-published his first novel, *Blue River,* but selling his book nearly cost him his life when his van fell into a lake in Oklahoma. However, when he woke up on the shore of that massive lake after his trip to the bottom of it in his van, he was truly awake for the first time in his young life. Not the kind of wakefulness that must climb mountains or conquer raging rivers; rather, Eddie had a deliberate and relaxed way of seeing and moving through his reality. And because of his awareness of presence, negative people and forces passed right through him.

Instead of writing his second novel, he left the van with his remaining one thousand copies of *Blue River* and his list of some eight thousand readers he'd sold to at the bottom of that lake. He had no desire to write again. Neither did he try to make a new life for himself. After "waking up," Eddie spent the past sixteen years living with his widowed mother in her mobile home in Council Bluffs, Iowa, across the river from Omaha where he worked nights driving a cab.

Eddie was a good son. He never complained about taking care of his mother's needs — grocery and medication runs, endless appointments with doctors, chauffeuring her back and forth in his cab to bingo and nursing homes to visit friends, and a monthly sixty-mile drive to Lincoln to visit his sister, Sara, and her family. Eddie's only vehicle was his cab, a white, 1986 Chevy Malibu. He had black magnetic signs on both doors advertising "Eddie's Cab" with his cell phone number.

Not long after waking up beside that lake, Eddie knew he had to keep his independence and do his own thing. That enervating experience of publishing and selling his own book until reaching his own inner peace — or what is best friend David had called "blue river" — had taught Eddie to work on his own terms, refusing to join the manswarm by depending on a salary he believed would take him back to unconsciousness. No way was Eddie Dense going back to that place.

Yes, Eddie was a different cat. A dozen years ago he'd taped a four-by-six card to his cab's visor that highlighted positive emotions he had to feel and acknowledge at least once every single shift he drove his cab. At least that was his conscious goal. He purposely worked nights from seven to three because he was interested in learning about his regulars — real characters who lived life on the edge — and far removed from the mundane routine at home with his mother.

Many of his regular customers were working alcoholics who had forfeited their driving privileges. They would tip Eddie well when dropped off sober at their favorite watering holes. Later, on the other side of his shift near closing time, Eddie would make his rounds ducking into several Omaha bars to pick up his rubber-legged regulars and shuttle them home. More often than not, he received another handsome tip.

Eddie had gotten the idea to serve the inebriated in this way while meditating at home for thirty minutes before and after his bartending shift at his parents' tavern in Council Bluffs. Serving alcohol to his parents' regulars had not agreed with his new consciousness, so it wasn't long before he was making more money in tips from driving a carload of patrons home than he was from tending bar for eight hours a night. Most importantly to Eddie, he was providing a positive service to the community. He felt good about that.

He credited his shift in consciousness to meditation. If not for sitting quietly focused on each breath for up to an hour a day, he knew he'd eventually slip back to a lower frequency of dulled senses — the same place he was in his youth before he left home in pursuit of inner peace after the tragic deaths of his two best friends. He also found meditation essential in order to stay alert while driving a cab all night. All kinds of characters were out at night, and E. L. Dense, author of one new-age novel, knew that there would be trouble if he was on their frequency.

When he gave up tending bar, Eddie told his mother, "It's killing my soul. I can't do it anymore." He put his energy into handing out business cards to other bartenders in the Council Bluffs-Omaha area. Before long, Eddie's cell phone was ringing in a steady stream of faces and a meaningful way to earn a living.

He had no desire to write a second book. He became interested in flipping down his visor and checking off the emotions he had to experience before his shift was over. An endless supply of hookers, drunks, drug addicts, gamblers, and all kinds of street people rode in the back of his cab and gave him enough images, dialog, and material to fill ten books. Eddie was just too busy living his life to write another book. Besides that, Eddie knew he didn't have another book in him like *Blue River*.

Then one night a strange coincidence happened. One of those little mysteries in everyone's life that reminds us we are all related in this web of confusion if we pay attention. One of Eddie's customers had left a copy of a worn paperback on his backseat floor, and Eddie found it the next day when he was gassing up. It was a Wallis Pond novel, his sixteenth book titled *The Impatient Man*. Right away Eddie recognized the Minnesota author as the same man who had sent him a letter over a decade and a half ago. Pond had written to E. L. Dense after reading his book *Blue River*. Eddie found out from Wallis Pond's letter how similarly they had marketed their books.

Reading *The Impatient Man* under his cab's dome light between fares, Eddie could see that Pond validated what Eddie had learned the hard way when selling his book. He had written, "Happiness depends on outer conditions perceived as positive ... but inner peace does not." For eleven nights Eddie read *The Impatient Man* between fares, taking in bits of wisdom here and there on page after page. He discovered that the sage author had also awakened after a near-death experience when flying his black vintage Monocoupe 70 — the very same popular high-performance small plane Charles Lindbergh had flown, and

"Lucky Lindy" could fly anything he wanted. Pond named his favorite plane "Superland" after his sales territory. He had the plane's name painted in bold orange, cursive lettering on both sides of the fuselage.

Eddie's fine orange hair tingled all around his skull as his remarkable imagination took in all of the details about Pond's precious V-braced, high-winged, radial-engine bird. It was nearly twenty feet long with a thirty-foot wingspan, and it had a cruising speed of one hundred miles per hour. The thrilling recount of the young aviator's flight one summer night in 1965 had Eddie glued to the book. Pond had been flying Superland in turbulent airspace and was running out of fuel above southwestern Minnesota near the South Dakota border. Because of the precarious winds and fuel situation, young Wallis was forced to make an emergency landing at night while descending fast and sputtering as he approached the little prairie town of Kenwick, Minnesota — the place the gypsy bachelor would eventually call home for the rest of his life.

While taking a short break from reading the book, Eddie removed the saved letter from his cab's glove box and saw that it was postmarked from Kenwick — the same tiny spot of earth where Pond had his life-changing, near-death experience. Again Eddie opened Pond's book and reread the incredible flying experience. He pored over every word and was able to see clearly what the author was saying:

> *I was still a young man and was becoming rich while in the throes of living my American Dream. Prosperity had given me the drive of four men; thus, I could never see myself settling in one place I would call home. I wanted to be everywhere ... see as many places and faces as I could. No one place was ever good enough for me.*
>
> *Riding the wings of Superland, I had the vantage point of a bird soaring above ten thousand places — truly seeing the lay of the land and how I should work it. I could never land and stay for long in one place because I knew that I would soon see another place that was more appealing to my restless soul. There! No,*

9

there! That's the place for me! This constant vacillation between permanence and motion got into my blood and made me the gypsy I was.

This kind of uncertainty about having a home went on for years and years. This jaded sense of doubt would diminish every place I saw. And this went on until I was flying Superland one summer night in 1965 en route to my hangar in Dakota Falls. I ran out of fuel because of such powerful headwinds I'd encountered since leaving Davenport at dusk. Gusting downdrafts had spiraled me down to five hundred feet as Superland choked for fuel as never before. I could see the web of streetlights of two small Minnesota towns but a few miles apart. I headed down for the blackness between them, hoping to find a stretch of isolated road to land on as my dying engine made intermittent bursts and halts. I had to quickly decelerate and descend while managing to stay above the tree line until I could see a suitable landing area where my fuselage had the best chance of sliding without breaking apart.

My headlight revealed open prairie that I knew was the only spot I had to land. I could see that the adjacent road that connected the towns had moving headlights in both directions, so landing there was not an option. The last thing I believed I would see in this world was a series of gullies and ravines coming at me at fifty miles per hour just before my wheels touched down.

For one instant I recall telling my Creator that I would settle down and never fly again if my life were spared. That's when I closed my eyes and raised my arms to shield my face for impact. I killed the engine and felt a horrific bounce. Miraculously, the thick prairie grass had slowed me until the plane spun around a few times and flipped over ever so slowly.

I was able to get out of the cockpit with only a few bumps and bruises. I stood there staring at my relatively undamaged airplane with its lone dimming

*headlight yet shining on this sacred patch of earth that
had spared me from a certain early death.*

*Dazed — but fully "awake" — I found myself
walking around this remarkable land until dawn,
thanking out loud every living thing for simply existing.
This humility and thankfulness was completely out of
character for me before my emergency landing. I knew
right then and there that this was where I would make
my home. I swore I would buy this ground no matter the
cost and as soon as possible. God, destiny, luck,
whatever it was ... I'd found my home. For the first time
in my life, every cell in my body was alive and in touch
with this organic essence of Being that was truly
committed to this land that I would name "Prairieville."*

*I had taken up flying in order to make money faster
and for the exhilaration flying can give a man who has
nobody to call "family." But this feeling was different.
I had made it to the other side where I was not just an
aging bundle of static atoms or thoughts. I was new
again ... and I could see it so clearly.*

Two independent writers — Wallis Pond and Eddie Dense
— had similar near-death experiences. Eddie had nearly
drowned, trapped with a thousand copies of his self-published
book inside his van that had settled upside-down on the bottom
of a massive lake in Oklahoma after a storm toppled it as it was
being ferried across the lake.

"To the other side," Eddie murmured under his dome light
upon finishing the book he had found in his cab. Unlike Pond,
Eddie chose to return home to a family he wanted to see in a
different light. Now Eddie wanted to find out all he could about
this prolific author who had sent him a letter asking him to sell
his last book to his loyal readers. *Why not just ship them out?
Why pay me big bucks to deliver them?* he wondered from
behind the wheel of his parked cab.

On the last page of the book in Eddie's hand was a clue —
a statement from Pond thanking his loyal readers in beauty shops
across the Midwest.

Over the next month, Eddie stopped into dozens of privately owned beauty shops in Omaha and Council Bluffs to find some of Wallis Pond's "loyal readers." They were independent business women who refused to sell or let the cab driver borrow one title from their collection of Wallis Pond novels that the beloved author had personally sold and autographed to them.

E. L. Dense had a list of over eight thousand readers inside his briefcase which was still on the bottom of that lake. Eddie's list was designed to do the same thing Wallis Pond had done — except Pond's plan to market his books was innately ingenious compared to Eddie's random sales to strangers. Answers to Pond's ingenious marketing were coming to Eddie at every Wallis Pond beauty shop Eddie could find in his area.

Coincidentally, Eddie found one of Pond's loyal readers at the same little beauty shop his mother had been going to for over twenty years, ever since she and her children moved into the mobile home Eddie called "FIKSHEN" in his novel *Blue River*. Eddie's mom had asked her hair stylist if her son could read her collection of Wallis Pond novels. The woman gave Eddie permission so long as he promised to be careful.

Book after book Eddie "carefully" read and returned — one per week and in publication sequence. Unbeknownst to Eddie, each title he read was warming him to the idea of marketing Mr. Pond's last book. Since each storyline pretty much took place in the same part of the country where Pond's readers worked and lived, Eddie was becoming more and more interested in seeing the places and faces Pond had described so masterfully. No longer did E. L. Dense feel he could only sell a book that he alone had authored. Besides, Wallis Pond's fiction was really about the author's life in sequence over twenty-six titles. Now Wallis Pond had gained one more loyal reader. Every night under the glow of his parked cab's dome light somewhere in Omaha sat a reader who really cared about what was going to happen to or what would be revealed about the author's leading character. And every reader knew the author's leading character was Wallis Pond himself.

Most people who met Wallis Pond were awed by his presence and magnetism. And just like self-published E. L.

Dense, Pond wrote extensively that he didn't want his books to be a part of the "great American sham that was validated by corporate bottom lines."

In America, there is a greasy flock of vultures in the publishing business waiting to swoop down and validate their next artist. If he or she happens to be an unconscious, drunken headline-maker with some talent, then he or she has the potential to be a household word they can feed on for as long as the public will swallow that kind of tripe. I will stay out of that sham that puts "having" ahead of "Being." I will be a different kind of writer, validating my own word by selling my books to my readers. Then I will know that I was not run by a vulture in a suit who decided to use me by foisting off my books to a reading public numb from and ignorant to this sham of all shams — this ugly part of my country that drowns in a toxic sea of green currency that purposely fools each new generation of consumers into believing that they have a choice in products that have proven to benefit them. Benefit whom?

I survived in a cold world of loveless parents and relied on my country's people to sustain me. I could see them all adopting "faster is better" and passing it on to their even lazier sons and daughters — all of whom wanted material things without effort and without pain. The lucky ones like me figured out that "having" things is not security or anything close to awareness of Being.

Sugar Daddy

What a pathetic sight he was now! Seventy-seven-year-old writer and businessman Wallis Pond was parked at his antique walnut roll-top writing desk while seated in his black motorized wheelchair — an expensive scooter with steering controls at the front of the right armrest. He was hunched forward at a forty-five-degree angle from advanced osteoporosis. Severe scoliosis and constantly aching knees kept him confined to his wheelchair most of the time. His purplish-brown tongue protruded from his salivating mouth. It had been swollen to the size of a cow's tongue after his second stroke, but now it was back to its normal size.

Despite his declining health and physical capabilities, he was at home on his beloved Prairieville. His readers knew his home was Prairieville because he wrote about it in all his novels since his emergency landing there in 1965. The house itself was seven thousand square feet, two stories tall with a basement, and constructed of Sioux quartzite from his property. The quartzite stones had been cut from the wall of rock that stood eighty yards to the south of the house and ran east and west for five hundred yards on Pond's 1,200 acres of wild prairie. The seventy-foot-high apex of the cliff line was not far from the front of the house and directly across from the old barn located on the southeast side of the house, fifty yards from the front door.

Both the cliff line and the exterior walls of the house had a rose-colored hue that sparkled after every rainfall. The house looked as if it could stand forever, along with the two rows of forty-foot-high massive oak trees running along the east and west sides of the house — likely as old as Wallis himself — that kept it completely shaded throughout the summer.

Wallis Pond self-published his first novel at the age of eighteen. As he started building and managing his famous beauty college, he published a novel every three or four years. After his retirement from Wallis Pond Beauty College, he poured himself into his writing and published a novel every other year. He never failed to write every day of his life, until his second stroke two years ago stopped him cold.

Every single day since his second stroke — the one the doctors said should have killed him — Wallis was hanging on, waiting for a stranger to visit him. With palsied hands that matched the color of his protruding tongue, he pulled out the letter sent to him over three months ago. Facing his large bay window at his desk that looked out onto the barn and splendid cliff line, he reread the letter. It was the words in the letter that were keeping him alive.

He sat in his darkened living room taking in the view of his beloved homestead. Behind him stood crooked, four-foot-high stacks of hardback books along nearly every inch of wall space. This room served as his library and office. Since he had moved his sleeping quarters to the main floor, he existed in his home without ever having to use the wheelchair pulley to go upstairs.

Books were Wallis Pond's life. They had made him wealthy. Locals in southwest Minnesota knew that the reclusive writer at Prairieville was the wealthiest man in four counties. His massive beauty college in Dakota Falls was funded at its inception by the words he'd penned with his right hand — a hand that was now atrophied and shaped like a lobster claw and utterly useless to him.

Gone were the "good ole days" when he had the energy of a tornado, peddling his early titles to thousands of beauty shops around Superland. Wallis was handsome then. He had taught himself how to live on nothing but his energy and good looks. Year after year he'd cover his route with a new book, selling them like gangbusters to women of all ages in beauty shops. And year after year his readers looked forward to the next title in the Wallis Pond series.

A Wallis Pond novel included his readers in every story. Whenever he entered a salon, all business would abruptly halt and all eyes were on him. He always talked to them one on one, inquiring about their lives and asking about their families. He often stopped mid-sentence to jot down a quick note in his notebook so he wouldn't forget what had just been said. His readers were flattered to think Wallis Pond was writing down words they had given him. They adored him.

Yes, he would write about their towns, the people they knew, and unusual things that happened that they were anxious to tell him about. All of the stories gleaned from the hardworking folks in Pond's Superland territory were put on the pages of book after book, and that absolutely delighted his growing loyal readership. Wallis Pond was like no other American writer because he validated the mundane lives of his readers as if they were a part of his family. And they were.

As he was working from salon to salon selling his third novel in his series, he got the idea to open his beauty college. He leased the first floor of what would become the Wallis Pond Building in downtown Dakota Falls — a city of 60,000 in 1957 and smack-dab in the middle of Superland.

Twenty-seven-year-old Wallis figured that people would get a haircut at least eight times a year, so he paid experienced stylists to train young future hair stylists in the art of cutting and styling hair. They also learned skills such as hair coloring, perms, manicures, pedicures, and even waxing. And unlike other schools, the students could start earning money while still attending school by cutting hair at a discounted rate. The beauty college, named after its founder, grew every year. Wallis Pond didn't stop at simply teaching skills and sending young stylists out into the world without a plan. Wallis knew the key to wealth was providing security for others who loved their work. He helped his graduates open salons in their communities by lending them the start-up costs on a five-percent-interest installment loan. He also had each borrower sign a contract agreeing to purchase Wallis Pond shampoos and conditioners, which were highest-quality products sold only in salons of Wallis Pond graduates.

What Wallis Pond really loved — and the thing that made him wealthy — was a simple verbal agreement between himself and every graduate: Every Wallis Pond graduate who owned and operated a salon would buy fifty signed copies of every Wallis

Pond novel at ten dollars a copy, then they would resell them to their customers. Eventually, that would peak to two thousand salons taking fifty copies each, or 100,000 books at ten dollars each. Wallis Pond was guaranteed revenues of one million dollars for every book he wrote from then on.

Wallis Pond — without advertising, without an agent, without a publisher or a distributor — was certainly the country's most popular unknown writer of his day. And best of all, his loyal readers loved his books.

Young Wallis spent his money on expensive toys, namely airplanes. He'd trade in and buy a new airplane like some people trade in for a new car every year. Every new book paid for his lavish lifestyle, including Prairieville and its 1,200 acres of wild prairie, and the home he would return to for rest and to write up a storm.

Wallis had no special woman in his life. He had many. Early on during his business's formative years, he'd made a vow to himself not to get involved romantically with any of his students, employees, graduates, or readers — all of whom loved Wallis Pond.

He kept his vow until he was nearly fifty-eight and beginning to decline in mobility from scoliosis and aching knees. The lifelong bachelor was no longer actively running his beauty college and was in the throes of a huge mid-life crisis. About that time a seventeen-year-old runaway farm girl from Madisonville walked into his beauty college. Marilyn Ditwell had the audacity to use Wallis Pond's name as a personal reference. She also had the nerve to apply for a management position as a floorwalker, which required an experienced stylist who would walk between the fifty-plus stations checking and critiquing the work done by each student.

When the broke, attractive, country girl with long brindle-colored hair was being interviewed, she didn't hesitate to lie to the interviewer. "Mr. Pond said to hire me right away for the floorwalker position," she asserted. When the personnel manager pressed Marilyn about not being informed by Mr. Pond that she should be hired, Marilyn said brusquely, "Call Mr. Pond right now and ask him. He said all I had to do was mention his name to you."

The interviewer was afraid to call her bluff, even though the girl only had a reference from a Madisonville salon where she worked part time for three summers. Marilyn Ditwell started work that day and was an excellent floorwalker from the beginning. She rented a studio apartment two blocks from work, and invested heavily in her clothing and appearance with each Wallis Pond paycheck she received.

It was a late spring day some three months later when the college was buzzing with the news that Wallis Pond was in the building. Marilyn had read most of his novels because she bought one every two weeks with each paycheck, and she really loved the Wallis Pond series of books. Wallis Pond novels were displayed on a revolving book rack in the front waiting area near the hair care products. Marilyn kept her books inside a bottom drawer in her desk at the back of the beauty college. She was prepared for and anticipating the day the boss would visit.

Excited to finally meet Wallis Pond, she combed her now-short hair at an empty station near her desk. She gathered up her collection and made her way down the long aisle between fifty-five busy students working on customers, hunting for the man who was now her favorite writer.

At five-foot-seven, 125 pounds, the attractive floorwalker was noticed right away by her boss, who could see that she was toting his books. He had sat down to rest his aching knees in his front waiting area. Just the short walk from his parking space to the front door convinced him that he was resigned to getting a walking cane.

"I love your books, Mr. Pond. Could you please sign my collection?" she asked with such sweet humility that he forgot how much his knees hurt.

He removed the pen he always kept in his shirt pocket. "Certainly," he smiled. He signed her books "To Marilyn" after reading his attractive floorwalker's name tag.

She sat next to him and handed him another book after each one he signed and handed back to her. "This is so wonderful.

You don't know how much your books entertained me when I first moved here. Thank you so much, Mr. Pond."

"Where are you from?" he asked her after handing her another signed book.

"Madisonville."

"A farm girl," he smiled.

"Well ... yeah ... but I hated it there ... and left as soon as I could. My parents wanted me to leave. So I learned how to cut hair at Betty's Boutique in Madisonville during summer breaks during high school. When things with my parents finally got bad enough, I ran away to Dakota Falls. I saw your ad for a floorwalker manager in the paper when I first got here, and I knew that was perfect for me ... just like it was my destiny. You know what I mean?" she smiled.

"Uh-huh," Wallis groaned as he took her last book to sign.

"In fact, Mr. Pond ... I prob'ly shouldn't maybe tell ya this ... but I sorta pulled one over during my interview for the job. I told Helen that you recommended me for the position. But I did a good job, Mr. Pond. Helen's real happy with me ... she told me. I know how to cut, style, and color hair, Mr. Pond, and I really needed this job so bad ... so I lied about you referrin' me. I hope I can keep workin' here now that I told you this," she winced adorably.

Wallis handed her the last book signed in his tornadic scrawl that she read out loud, "To my favorite floorwalker, Marilyn. Thanks for your creative energy. Wallis Pond."

She was touched and dipped her head to the stack of books on her lap to hide the tears filling her eyes.

"Marilyn," he whispered.

She looked up into the smiling gray eyes of her boss.

"I would enjoy it immensely if I could take you to lunch now," Pond smiled.

She blinked as if not believing what she heard.

"What time do you go to lunch, Marilyn?" He checked his expensive watch. "It's about eleven now," he said. He then directed his words to one of his receptionists. "Jody?"

"Yes, sir," Jody smiled so wide-eyed that it tickled Marilyn.

"Please have Helen come to the waiting area."

She took off so fast that Marilyn giggled at her boss's power. Helen arrived fast, smiling down at her seated boss.

"Helen, I want to thank you for hiring my friend Marilyn. I want to take her to lunch now so we can discuss some ideas she has about this place. Will you please arrange for someone to cover for her ... on the clock ... so we can be on our way?"

"Certainly, Mr. Pond. No problem. I'll handle everything."

"Thank you, Helen."

Marilyn was thrilled and stunned while carrying her signed books back to her desk. She quickly grabbed her modest handbag, dabbed a hint of Elizabeth Taylor's Passion behind each ear and onto her wrists, and touched up her hair with a brush at the same empty station. He told her he'd be waiting in his car.

Every morning Marilyn walked to work because she had no other mode of transportation. Now she was having lunch with Wallis Pond. *What will I even say?* she wondered. *And the way he covered for me with Helen ... that was so nice of him.* Then she recalled a chapter from one of his books where there was an age difference between two romantically attracted characters. She giggled when she recalled that he wrote, "Age is mind over matter: If she don't mind ... it don't matter."

Marilyn Ditwell from Madisonville felt like a queen riding in Wallis Pond's new black Mercury to an upscale downtown restaurant only a few blocks from his beauty college. She wanted to show her boss that age didn't matter to her. It was when he parked and had great difficulty getting out of his car that she saw her opportunity. She hurried to his side, locked her arm into his, and patiently matched his turtle pace mandated by his aching knees. When he grumbled to her that he was getting old and should get a cane, she surprised him and said, "I think you'd look incredibly distinguished with a cane. But it has to be the right cane. After all ... you are a famous writer. So it must be a cane that matches your accomplishments, don't you think?" she asked seriously.

Wallis chuckled, then really laughed hard for the first time in a very long time. And his pain was more bearable with her arm helping to steady his walk into the restaurant.

She had her first-ever prime rib dinner, medium-rare like his, and her first-ever martini without being carded. He talked more than he had in years and realized the young woman was mature and knew how to listen. To Wallis she appeared to act as if in her thirties with her poised and serious demeanor. When he asked her how old she was — after ordering a second martini — she lied again, just as she had to get hired at his beauty college. "How old do you think I am?" she smiled.

"Oh, I'm so bad at that. Just tell me your age," he chuckled.

"I'm twenty-seven," she lied with a smile.

"Twenty-seven?" the skeptical writer replied with a raised eyebrow. "So you ran away from the farm at twenty-seven?" the silver-haired Pond tilted his head slightly.

"That's my story," she hiccuped, and they both laughed. Then she coyly added, "Age is mind over matter ... right?"

Pond smiled knowing she had read that in his book.

After lunch they found a men's clothing store a few doors south of the restaurant. She picked out the most expensive walking cane made of cherry wood, which was perfectly suited for his six-foot-two frame. He used the cane as he walked to his Mercury, yet she held onto his free arm even though he'd switched his cane over to the other hand to ease his weight on his knees when stepping down from the curb.

"Does it help?" she asked once inside his car.

"Yes ... and so does the cane," he smiled into her eyes.

From that day on, Wallis would pick up his "twenty-seven-year-old" floorwalker every day for lunch. He would patiently wait in his car at his parking space for her. For the first time, Wallis had broken his vow to never date one of his employees. For three months their relationship was platonic. Wallis would buy her clothes in the city's most chic women's clothing stores. He also bought her jewelry and her first new car — a white Cadillac — just two weeks after they became lovers in his Prairieville home one Saturday night.

Within three months of deepening their relationship and three months shy of her nineteenth birthday, she was pregnant. The news floored both of them because Marilyn didn't want to become a mother, nor Wallis a father. Sensitive Wallis talked her out of having an abortion and agreed to support the child until he or she was eighteen if she found a good home for the child. The thousand-dollar monthly child support check was paid on time by Pond's accountant and mailed to Marilyn, who would forward it to the farm. The money sent to her parents was the only reason Ned and Bert agreed to raise her "illegitimate" child.

It was all arranged two months before she delivered Mickey Ditwell. Because of his loyal readership, Pond insisted that the boy keep his mother's name. Marilyn was fine with that because her boyfriend-boss had bought her a loft apartment in the historical district of downtown Dakota Falls. Mickey Allen Ditwell was the name his mother gave him. She liked the name after a nurse told her the baby had protruding round ears like Mickey Mouse.

No nursing her baby; Marilyn Ditwell didn't want to ruin her breasts. Wallis never saw his son or ever tried to, fearing he'd see some resemblance and become attached. He had his negative doubts whether the boy was his son, since Marilyn said she dated "a bunch of guys" before she met Wallis. But he took her word for it because he didn't want any evidence from a blood test.

Wallis had all but abandoned his son, just as his father had done to him. The successful writer and businessman had other reasons for not wanting to be in Mickey's life. Even though Marilyn remained working at Wallis Pond, their relationship as lovers ended. She remained in close contact with her boss and used him many times when she wanted money. He would buy her new tires for her car and give her money for trips she'd take "alone."

It was all done in friendship, though Wallis feared a paternity suit that would ruin his image as a writer. The protagonist in all of his books was Billy Lake, an abandoned boy who spent his life searching for the parents who had deserted him. In every storyline, Billy was the author's alter ego — a flawed character who never failed to do the right thing. Billy would help others who came into the world without a parent to love or nurture them. Billy Lake would lead the way, giving hope and comfort in ways that touched his readers so much that it made them crave more of the incredible Billy Lake.

The man Wallis Pond was very generous. He donated five thousand dollars every year for ten years to the Dakota Falls Boys and Girls Home. He gave twenty thousand several times to a shelter for unwed mothers in the city. He arranged for and financed loans for hundreds of his beauty college graduates to open their own salons in hundreds of small Midwest towns and cities.

Known for being an "easy touch" for anyone in trouble, many times this altruistic man would do things for people without any publicity, even if they didn't work for him. At least a dozen times a year, someone he'd heard about who was having trouble would be surprised to find out their hospital bills or travel expenses were paid by an anonymous benefactor. Yes, Wallis Pond was no taker. He was just a good man who never married and had no reason or knowhow to be a parent.

His mother had come through on his birthday. Mickey was so used to getting a check on this day that he hadn't even bothered opening the envelope when he brought in the mail and slapped it onto the table for Bert and Ned to pore over like vultures. When Mickey opened the envelope, he was surprised to see his biggest birthday check ever — five hundred dollars! He noticed how his rheumy-eyed grandparents were curious to know just how much their daughter had sent him. For all intents and purposes, this was Mickey's last month to live under their roof. Wallis Pond's August child support check was the last money they'd get for rooming and boarding his "bastard son."

Right away the birthday boy got on his old black Stingray bicycle and pedaled toward town some two miles away on gravel roads. Bert and Ned never would allow him to buy a guitar and play it in the house. They always told him that when he was eighteen, he could do whatever he wanted — after he moved out.

He knew he wanted to buy a black Gibson guitar and an amplifier, and he had a catalog picture of them inside his black cowhide wallet along with his driver's license and the big check from his mother.

Mickey's six-foot-two, string-bean frame looked silly on his bike. His long legs would rise with each slow revolution to his slouched-over upper body. His pencil neck craned forward and his hands and arms raised up to grip his high handlebars. He looked like some apathetic home-schooled hick who just turned eighteen and knew everything he needed to know on this very special day.

Like his mother, he was home-schooled by Mrs. Flett in her home three farms west of the Ditwell farm. Mickey had two female classmates who would also be starting their senior year in two weeks, but Mickey had other plans.

As he slowly side-winded down the gravel road under the hazy, late-morning August sun, he went over his plan. After all, he carried the genes of Wallis Pond, so he carefully rehearsed the speech he had prepared for the manager of The Music Store, who had seen him many times eyeing the guitar and amp. *I'll show him my check and tell him I'll give him four hundred for the guitar and amp after I cash it ... if he throws in a case for the guitar. And when he reminds me that the price is $489 ... I'll leave and tell him I'll buy it in Dakota Falls.* That was Mickey Ditwell's plan — and it worked like a charm because the store manager was hungry for a sale.

Even though the bank teller knew the Ditwells and didn't ask their grandson for his ID, Mickey removed his license from his wallet and showed it to her. He wanted to show someone that he was eighteen now. Free at last!

"How come the flag is at half-staff?" he asked the teller after she counted out the four requested one-hundred-dollar bills and five twenties.

"A soldier from Pierre was killed in Iraq yesterday."

She could see he had a little smirk on his lips. And when he stuffed his money into his wallet he said dryly to her, "I guess it could've been worse."

"How's that?" The teller would soon wish she hadn't asked.

"He could've had his arms or legs blown off ... and lived."

His words creeped her out, but it was his God-awful laugh that made the hairs on the back of her neck stand up until she had to scratch them back down.

Leaving the bank, Mickey stopped and looked up at Old Glory flapping its fabric in the stiff prairie wind South Dakota is known for. He thought about that soldier and how he probably wasn't much older than himself. Mickey vowed, *They ain't gettin' me to die over there for those ingrates.* Then he folded his arms in front of himself and said silently to the flag, *I happen to believe patriotism and nationalism are dangerous ... especially to guys my age. I don't want to die for an American corporation and rich white men who would never die for me. It's poor guys my age who can't get their hands on enough money with a good-paying job at home who die over there.*

25

People who stand behind the flag take your little boys to church every Sunday and teach them to believe that killing is a sin ... a sin you will go to hell for. Old Glory ... I read that on D-Day when young American soldiers were in the heat of battle and ordered to fire at the Germans defending the beaches, that only one in twenty-five of your soldiers could actually fire their weapons because they found it so hard to kill another human being. So your army learned to dehumanize the enemy by labeling them as targets, barbarians, attackers ... that them-versus-us baloney. Flag, I'm gonna buy me a guitar and amp with my money and ride away from you and say, "Better you than me, buddy ... better you than me."

On his way back to The Music Store he reminded himself that "small is tall." Each and every step he took from now on was a part of the journey that would get him to his goal: Freedom.

For eighteen years Mickey Ditwell had purposely stayed small by not making any friends or speaking many words to anyone, like he'd just done in the bank. But from now on, things would be different. For starters, the teller in the bank had told all five bank employees what the "Ditwell boy" had said to her, and those five people would spread the word to the whole town within twenty-four hours, validating to them all that the Ditwell boy was ... different.

Soon Mickey had his guitar and amp with free guitar case. He handle-looped it around his left handlebar and awkwardly steered his bike with his left hand while laboriously holding the amp by its handle with his right hand. He had to pedal slowly to keep his balance on the Main Street sidewalk until he spotted a familiar old pickup parked in front of the Madisonville Doo Drop Inn.

He got off his bike and carefully set his amp down after leaning his bike against the front wall of the bar. He walked over to the truck and smiled upon seeing the key still in the ignition. Quickly he loaded his bike, amp and guitar into the truck's bed and drove it away.

Fifteen minutes later, after delivering his amp and guitar to the farm, he returned the truck to the same parking space. He left the key in the ignition and off-loaded his bike, then pedaled slowly back to the farm.

Yesterday he wouldn't have done such a thing. Today was different.

* * * * *

Two weeks after Mickey's birthday, the last child support check was in its final days and Mickey needed wheels. Ned and Bert would never let their grandson drive their old Buick — their only vehicle — to school, let alone out into the world. "Lord knows he'd find trouble," Bert would rail at her reticent husband.

So the last Saturday in August — before even old Harold the rooster was up — Mickey took the Buick and his remaining one hundred dollars and drove to Dakota Falls. His clothes, bike, guitar and amp all fit inside the car's deep trunk.

In downtown Dakota Falls, he parked the stolen car under a viaduct by the Big Sioux River not far from the post office. Black jeans, black T-shirt and black Nikes moved along the sidewalk like a walking toothpick. An all-black baseball cap shielded his light-gray eyes from the rising sun that would soon be too hot for the all-black attire he always wore whenever he came to the city.

He had told Bert he would leave the farm when he turned eighteen and go to Kenwick to meet his half-sister, Katie, for the first time. But Bert knew that Wallis Pond also lived in Kenwick, and that was Mickey's main intention — to meet his father for the first time.

He walked close to the river and stopped to gaze up at the replica statue of Michelangelo's *David* as a large flock of great Canadian geese nibbled grass nearby. To the east was the curving viaduct he'd later drive over to reach the tattoo shop, but his attention was focused to the west on the large two-story Wallis Pond Building.

As he started to walk toward the beauty college, Mickey was lost in his reverie of the last time he saw his mother.

Marilyn Spink had been managing the Wallis Pond Beauty College for several years, but it would soon be closing its doors for good after thirty-two years of training nearly ten thousand stylists to be independent professionals and business managers.

It was the morning of Mickey's seventeenth birthday. A new white Cadillac had parked outside the Ditwell farmhouse and honked once for the birthday boy to come out.

The night before, Mickey had overheard heated words coming from behind Ned and Bert's closed bedroom door. "He stops sendin' those checks, and I'll boot his ass off the farm right quick!" Ned had barked to his wife.

When seventeen-year-old Mickey approached the black-tinted windows of the white Cadillac and saw the personalized license plate "CADMAN," he knew this was not his father. Rather, alone in his luxury car was Marv Larson, the Cadman, who extended his tanned right hand after Mickey had opened the back passenger door. His mother wasn't there but had sent the silver-haired, rich car dealer to pick him up.

The Cadman was nice enough, explaining how he was taking Mickey to a restaurant in Dakota Falls to meet up with his mother for a birthday lunch. "So it's your seventeenth birthday. How's it feel to be another year older?"

"Good," Mickey mumbled. Then he said to himself, *Just great, Cadman. I'm home-schooled out here in the sticks and socially retarded. But aside from that ... it sucks.*

Mickey kept quiet for most of the drive, looking down at the black grease under his fingernails from changing his bike's chain. Then his self-talk continued, *It feels like I hate the world a little more today. But thanks for askin'.*

He had gone a year without a haircut. His brindle-colored hair was long and touching his shoulders. Knowing there was a slight chance he might get to see his father, he secretly agreed to allow his mother to cut his hair at the beauty college.

The Cadman sat in the Wallis Pond waiting area as Marilyn the manager personally shampooed, cut and styled her son's hair. At thirty-six, his mother was in the prime of her physical beauty. Her hair was ash-blonde — a shade lighter than her natural brindle color that matched her son's. Mickey watched as long strips of his hair fell to the tile floor beneath the swirling barber chair as the lightning-fast scissors did their job.

Any student who cut hair slowly was in early training and, subsequently, would give a lousy cut. Marilyn Spink was fast and good. Mickey was impressed that she was the boss who went around to each station to critique each head that was swivelled to face the aisle whenever the haircut was completed by the student.

When Mickey's haircut was finished, he opened his eyes to see in the mirror that she had given him the same conservative, college-boy haircut the Cadman had. He pretended to like it. "I might as well like it," he answered his mother's inquisitive stare in the station's mirror.

Marilyn took her son and Marv to the same downtown restaurant where she'd had her first lunch with Mickey's father. Alone in the restaurant's restroom, Mickey wanted to punch his new reflection in the mirror. Then he returned to his mother's table and to that rich guy he wished wasn't there.

At his place setting was a birthday card with a check for three hundred dollars inside. The card was signed, "Love, Mom."

"Thanks," he said to his mother.

"What're you gonna do with all that money?" the red-faced car dealer laughed as he finished his second bourbon and Coke.

"I'm savin' for a guitar and a tattoo."

"Oh, Mickey ... don't tell me you're going to mark your body with those things. They'll always be there," his mother protested.

"Aw, Mom ... c'mon," the Cadman said in Mickey's defense. "All the kids are gettin' 'tooed."

"What exactly will be your tattoo?" Marilyn asked with reluctant resignation.

"I want a red hammer," he pointed just below his shoulder on his upper arm.

"A red hammer? What for?" Marilyn pressed her son.

He shrugged his shoulders, not wanting to explain. When Mickey reached for his Coke, his mother saw something else she didn't like. She put down her vodka and tonic and reached for Mickey's free hand to examine his fingernails.

"Look at those black nails! When we get back to the shop, I'm going to give you a manicure." That was okay with Mickey. It would give him another chance to see his father — maybe.

Now, as he walked up to the front door of the beauty college, he was surprised to find it was out of business. Closed for good. And there wasn't anyone around to ask what happened to the once-thriving business. He pressed his face to the glass and looked inside. Nothing. All the station chairs were gone; the place was empty.

A hundred thoughts bombarded his mind, including his biggest fear — that his father had died before he could meet him.

He walked fast toward the river where he'd parked Ned and Bert's car.

Kenwick

Mickey still had half a tank of gas when he crossed the state line into Minnesota on I-90. He breathed a sigh of relief that he hadn't been picked up by the Highway Patrol in South Dakota.

Sixteen miles into Minnesota, Mickey turned north at the LeRoy exit onto the road that, according to the open map on the Buick's front seat, would take him to Kenwick. He hoped the drive wouldn't be too long since it was starting to get hot inside the car. Ned was too tight to have the car's air conditioning system recharged with Freon.

Kenwick was small — a hick town that was much smaller than Madisonville. He found it incredible that his sister and father could live in such a dinky town. The tallest building in Kenwick was the Farmers Elevator at the end of the three-block-long Main Street. The town hall was across the street from the one-room post office. Next to the post office was Kenwick's only bar. A small volunteer fire station was next door to the little grocery store, Bing's Grocery. The thought of food made him think of Ned and Bert. He was sure by now they had the law searching for him.

Not a soul was walking the streets of Kenwick, so he cruised around looking for the address on Kenwick Road where his sister lived. He had memorized the address from birthday and Christmas cards he'd received from his mother when she was still living in Kenwick. It didn't take him long in the small town to find the beige one-story house belonging to the Spinks, but there were no cars parked in the driveway. He parked in a shady spot in front of the one-stall garage and listened for any signs of life in or around the house. Nothing.

His gray eyes saw a girl's purple bike on the grass in front of the house. *Katie's bike*, he thought.

His right upper arm itched from the tattoo he'd gotten before leaving Dakota Falls. He raised his right T-shirt sleeve onto his shoulder and adjusted the rearview mirror to have a look at his four-inch-high red hammer. The tattoo was the beginning of his pledge to himself to hammer out one song that he alone would create with his new Gibson inside Ned's trunk.

It wasn't even noon yet, and already Mickey Ditwell had done more to change his life than in all of his eighteen previous years. He reclined the driver's seat and stayed behind the wheel in the shade to avoid the glaring August sun. Thinking about how angry Ned would be at losing his car gave Mickey a headache in both temples.

After closing his eyes for about ten minutes, he heard behind him the rumbling wheels of something being pulled on the blacktop of Kenwick Road. He sat up and readjusted the rearview mirror to see a short, stocky, dark-complected young man about his own age pulling an olive-green aluminum wagon that appeared to have wings.

Mickey got out of the car and waved at the lone pedestrian. He was muscular and wore only denim cut-offs and ragged, dirty, green tennis shoes. He had a muscular neck like the jocks Mickey had seen in Madisonville.

Johnny Apple was naturally friendly, yet leery of someone wearing all black on such a hot day. *He must know the Spinks,* Johnny surmised to himself while standing on the desolate road.

As he walked over to Johnny, Mickey was stunned to see what was inside the wagon. A large, untethered, cinnamon-brown hawk about fourteen inches tall with sharp talons was clutching at the back of the wagon. Inside the wagon was a radio-controlled, partially assembled, yellow model airplane and assorted tools, all of which intrigued Mickey.

"You fly that?" Mickey asked.

"Yep," Johnny smiled.

"You gonna fly it now?"

"Yep."

"Mind if I watch?"

"If ya want."

"Sweet!"

They walked along the blacktop on the left side facing what little oncoming traffic they encountered.

"You know the Spinks?" Johnny asked.

"Not really. Marilyn's my mom."

"Oh ..." Johnny said, as if he knew something about this stranger's mother that he shouldn't mention.

"I guess nobody's home," Mickey said while looking back in the direction of the Spink house.

"Mr. Spink takes Katie to the matinee in LeRoy every Saturday."

"Where did you get that bird? Is it a hawk?"

"Yeah ... a red-tailed hawk. My dad and I found it in a nest over there," Johnny pointed to the trees off to their right. "A couple of idiots killed her mother and I raised it. Her name's Lucky."

"Lucky ... That's a perfect name for her. How come she doesn't fly away?"

"She won't unless I launch her."

"Really? Sweet! My name's Mickey, by the way."

"Johnny."

"Johnny and Lucky goin' flyin'. Yer both lucky."

"Yeah ... You say Mrs. Spink is yer mom?"

"Yeah ... But I haven't seen her in a year. I lived on a farm in Madisonville, South Dakota."

"You haven't talked to her in a year?" Johnny asked in disbelief.

"Nope. She never raised me. She got pregnant when she was young and decided she didn't want to take care of me."

"Wow. What about yer dad?"

"He lives around here ... somewhere."

"In Kenwick?"

"Yeah."

"So yer dad isn't Karl Spink, Katie's dad?"

"No. Wallis Pond is my dad."

"Wallis Pond is your dad?" Johnny asked with such incredulity that he stopped pulling his wagon.

"Yeah. Why?"

"He's, like, the richest guy around here! That's where I'm goin' now to fly my plane ... to his place ... Prairieville!"

"Prairieville?"

Johnny pointed to the land across the road on their right. "That's the name of his land ... his homestead. It's over a thousand acres. You've never been there?"

"Nope ... And I've never met him."

Going to the very home of the man who had never claimed him as a son was not where Mickey had intended on going so soon after arriving in Kenwick, but he continued on and raised his sleeve to examine his tattoo that itched like crazy.

"What'd ya get 'tooed on yer arm?" Johnny stopped to more closely examine the red hammer. "Cool," he said.

"I just got it," Mickey replied.

As they continued on Johnny asked, "What does the hammer mean?"

"Red represents my passion for my music. And the hammer means persistence pounding out my music. To me it means never giving up on my passion to create music."

"I'll get 'tooed after I graduate next May," Johnny said.

"Why wait?"

"My dad won't let me get one till I'm outta his house."

"I know what ya mean," Mickey commiserated.

"I'm passionate about flying. My dad says it's my only vice," the young pilot chuckled proudly.

"Sweet."

Mickey's gray eyes raked over the contents of the wagon. He had the same gift his father had — the ability to see things, even the little things that filled the pages of twenty-six novels. He noticed the yellow converted glider with blue trim, the black toolbox that was dented and faded as if it had been used for twenty years, a folded tarp tucked tightly beside a brown paper bag that appeared to be a sack lunch, some kind of fuel container wedged purposely between the toolbox and the side of the wagon, and a twenty-four-ounce plastic bottle of water that was still partially frozen. The sight of the sweating water bottle made the stranger in black so thirsty that he asked if he could "take a swig of that water."

After a long drink, Lucky's brown-and-gold eyes were on him, surveying the human as if unafraid.

"So yer name's Mickey Pond?" Johnny asked.

"No ... Ditwell. That was my mom's name before she married Karl Spink."

"Have you met Karl?"

"Nope. My mom divorced Karl and lives with this rich car dealer in Dakota Falls."

As they approached the gated entrance to Prairieville, Lucky stretched her thirty-six-inch wingspan on her moving perch as if knowing she would fly soon with the yellow bird riding next to her.

"My dad works for Mr. P." Johnny said. "He told my dad that yer mom left Karl so she could drive a new car every year. Karl didn't have enough money for her. That's what Mr. P said."

"That sounds about right," Mickey agreed.

"Mr. P was so upset when she left Karl and Katie that he closed his beauty college for good. Mr. P said he only kept the place open 'cause she needed the job. He told my dad she'd never get another dime from him." After a short pause Johnny asked his walking companion, "Did you come here to see your mom?"

"Not really."

"Karl quit his job as an ice cream salesman. Now that his wife's gone, he had to get a job at the elevator in town so he can be close to home ... 'cause he has to raise Katie all by himself."

Off to their right was a long stand of forty-foot-tall scraggly pines and blue spruce that lined Prairieville's eastern border. Along the tree line was a barnwood fence that was kept in good condition by Johnny's father.

"I usually fly earlier in the day before it gets too hot ... or at the end of the day when the wind is more unpredictable."

"Lat. 44," Mickey said.

"What do you mean?" Johnny asked.

"Latitude 44 degrees. You'll learn all about it when you fly real planes. It's this imaginary series of lines that run east-west all around the globe. We're at latitude 44 degrees. I read somewhere that winds get charged with some kind of magnetic energy when they blow across the Badlands at lat. 44. That's why I bought my guitar ... to tap into that energy and create something never heard before in this airspace."

"That's interesting."

Mickey was reminding Johnny of "Mr. P" by talking about creating something that was all his. Words like "charged" and "energy" were often used by the old writer when he talked to Johnny about his flying days when he was a young man.

Lloyd Apple was secretly proud of his son, yet he never told his son he was proud of him like Mr. P would often do. Lloyd's words usually focused on what Johnny was doing wrong.

"Maybe you could stay here ... live at Prairieville with your dad," Johnny said.

"I was an accident he didn't want. He's not gonna want me around to remind him of that."

"Maybe not ... but he's an old man now in a wheelchair, and he lives alone in a big house. He might want some company."

"I doubt it. ... He's in a wheelchair?"

"Yeah. He gets around pretty good, though."

The swinging black aluminum gate was open, as it usually was. Johnny pulled his wagon past the gate with Mickey close behind. Gradual up-sloping prairie hills surrounding a circuitous one-lane blacktop road obstructed any view. Prairieville was well over a thousand acres of private land and one of Minnesota's rare unprotected grassland preserves.

Underlying most of Prairieville was a massive outcrop of rock known as Sioux quartzite — a pink-hued rock that was used in most commercial building in the upper Midwest and most of the paved roads and highways. As they climbed the single-lane blacktop drive, Mickey noticed the surrounding bulbous prairie hills were covered by a billowy waving sea of green-gold summer grasses. In some places the grass grew as high as six feet, but in many places the blue-violets of the purple prairie clover were visible.

The winds over Prairieville were incredible. Swirling gusts and breezes seemed to drop the temperature some ten degrees and brought relief to the boy in black, who feared meeting the man who owned all of this incredible land.

They reached the apex of the lane, and three hundred yards ahead lay the heart of Prairieville: the two-story, quartzite, fortress-like home of Wallis Pond. The old gray barn was off to the right and a ways in front of the house. The looming seventy-foot-high cliff line — a sheet of massive Sioux quartzite moved here by glaciers millions of years ago — stretched for five hundred yards to the south of the house.

The cliff line sloped lower toward where the two visitors were standing. Johnny carried his diesel-powered, converted single-cylinder glider up a worn path that led to his launching pad at the highest point on the cliff line. This was the perfect wide-open place to fly his planes by radio sound waves. Mickey was busy thinking of the music he could make in this place.

When they reached the entrance to the path, Mickey watched Johnny kneel beside his wagon, remove a utility knife from his toolbox, and trim off an ever-so-tiny sliver of balsa wood from the plane's belly before filing it smooth with a piece of steel wool. The young aviator did this all from experience because he knew how the wind and late-August air pressure would affect his wing lift. To himself Johnny said, *Lift equals weight and thrust equals drag.*

"Do you think he's home?" Mickey asked while staring at the shaded house.

"He's always home," Johnny scoffed upon spilling a few drops of fuel as he filled the glider's tank.

"He doesn't mind if you fly here?"

"Naw ... He says I can fly here anytime I want. That's what he told my dad."

Just then Mickey had an idea — or a good reason — to talk to the man who had sent Ned and Bert a grand a month for the past eighteen years.

Johnny adroitly attached the wings to the yellow bird and carried his assembled plane and handheld remote control box up the sloping grassland path toward the cliff line. Lucky stayed on her perch in the wagon, watching her trainer like a hawk.

Mickey scratched his red hammer and followed Johnny after grabbing the bottle of iced water and taking another swig. His eyes were focused on the long wheelchair ramp leading up to the front door of the house.

Inside the house, silver-haired, seventy-seven-year-old Wallis Pond was seated in his wheelchair at his cherry wood roll-top desk. Facing his front bay window that looked out to his cliff line, he felt tired and trapped in the shadows of age.

Again, Wallis wanted to read the letter he had received several weeks before from the writer in Council Bluffs whom Wallis had first contacted over a decade and a half ago. He had asked the fledgling writer if he would be interested in ghostwriting and marketing Wallis Pond's "last novel" to his loyal readers. At the time he wrote the letter, Wallis Pond truly intended his eighteenth novel to be his last. But the former aviator's inspiration and ambition never left him, despite his advancing years. Wallis Pond kept creating and publishing his novels up to his seventieth birthday.

Eddie Dense had called Wallis Pond shortly after receiving the letter and had agreed to meet with him to discuss the storyline and marketing plan. But the day before their scheduled meeting, Eddie's mother had fallen and broken her hip. When the doctor advised that she needed hip-replacement surgery and would require several months of physical therapy afterward, Eddie knew he had to indefinitely postpone his meeting with Wallis Pond in order to care for his aging mother. The senior writer, although envious of the relationship between Eddie and his mother, understood the younger writer's position and agreed to postpone the meeting. Neither of them knew at the time it would be sixteen years and nine novels later before they would finally meet.

Sitting in his library, Wallis again read the letter he'd read once a day since receiving it. He knew it was this letter that kept him alive.

Dear Mr. Pond:

Considerable time has passed since we last spoke about your offer to write and market your last book. I'm not sure if you still are interested in pursuing this project, but I thought I'd give you a little bit more information about myself in case you are.

At the time I received your letter, I had just ended my door-to-door selling of Blue River *— some 9,000 copies. I was burnt out, to say the least. After my mother's hip replacement, my father died and it was up to me to support my mother. I spent many years caring for her and letting time heal me without ever writing another word that I cared to publish.*

Since our last contact, I have read every one of your twenty-six novels, thanks to one of your loyal readers in a Council Bluffs beauty shop. I am not only impressed with your writing, I am amazed at the remarkable way your beauty college students became your loyal readers. It's ingenious, Mr. Pond, how you marketed your books.

When your "loyal reader" here told me about how your health was failing, my intrigue about your mysterious and long-awaited last book made me want to write to you. You have said over and over in your books that "there's nothing quite as beautiful as mystery." Because I know you were the protagonist William "Billy" Lake in all of your stories, I have come to know you as a man who lived, loved, and lost as no other man I know of.

I know you were abandoned by your parents and left alone in this world to find your way. You must still be at Prairieville, for you wrote in your last novel, "I will die here a lonely man and not be understood until my last book is read and I'm gone."

I have not written another novel since Blue River *and know not whether you ever finished your last book — or whether your generous offer for me to sell it to your readers is still on the table. Something tells me I should help you get your last book out into a world that I also feel needs to read it in order to understand your incredible life as an American novelist.*

I plan to drive up from Council Bluffs to visit you as soon as I clear up some of my mother's business here. Regardless, I intend to meet my favorite writer.

    Sincerely,

      Eddie Dense

Severely arthritic and crippled Wallis Pond removed his tinted, oval-shaped reading glasses. He cast his cloudy gray eyes over to the stack of 360 typed pages of his last book wrapped in clear plastic on the right-hand upper corner of his desk. The manuscript's title was in bold, black letters. *Superland* had been recently amended and cleaned up by his lifelong editor, Mrs. Thistlethwaite — a widowed, retired librarian who lived in LeRoy just two miles away.

Atop the cliff line, Mickey handed Johnny the bottle of iced water. After a drink, Johnny saw a pair of hawk-skittish rock doves soaring above Prairieville. The birds would be shot by microbursts of air that would catapult them higher with such ferocity that he thought he could do Cuban eights after a few slow rolls in wind like this. It made him wish that his dad were there to see him fly in such conditions.

But Lloyd Apple was perched on his barstool behind the tinted windows of the Kenwick Tavern just two blocks from the Apple home. He was gulping down his first cold beer and watching the Twins game while his wife, Maxine, ironed clothes all afternoon.

The old man, wearing khaki shorts with pockets full of medication, cursed "the chair" when he bumped his aching knee on the corner of his desk as he tried to reach up and twist open the front window blind. His doctor in Dakota Falls said he should have both knees replaced. "No way! You're not sawing through my bones; I'd rather live in a wheelchair!" And so he does.

He felt below his kneecap to see if it was bleeding, since being on a blood thinner meant he could bleed to death. He knew the chair had weakened his heart because of the tingling sensation in his feet and hands. Plus his heart was out of rhythm.

From his chair behind his desk, he scoffed at his right writing hand for not being able to write a legible word. It was covered with blue veins and brown liver spots, and it was the only "good hand" he could use to raise the binoculars to his eyes.

From his bay window with the aid of binoculars, he could see clearly that another boy was with Johnny on his cliff line — and that he was dressed in black on such a hot day. He also could see Johnny kneeling next to his glider, focused on squeezing drops of fuel into the plane's exhaust parts while holding a finger over the air intake. His father had taught him to do this while turning the propeller a few times counter-clockwise to prime and start his engine.

On the cliff line, Mickey watched Johnny cover his forearm with a thick cotton arm pad his mother had made for him to use when flying Lucky. Johnny kissed the air in the direction of his parked wagon. At the sound of the high-pitched kissing noise, the hawk instantly left her perch and made a beeline for Johnny. She landed gently on her trainer's extended forearm.

"Sweet!" Mickey exclaimed. "How did you teach her to stay on the wagon and come to you like that? That's so cool."

"It's the only command I've ever used ... and I'd use it every time I fed her."

Lucky's regal hood cocked and turned to Johnny when he made the kissing sound again and handed her birdseed from his pocket. She pecked from his palm without touching his skin with her raptor-like, butterscotch-colored, curved beak that could tear flesh to pieces.

"Red-tailed hawks like to sit on telephone poles and watch for rodents. Mr. P told me that."

Johnny stepped up to the edge of the cliff line and launched Lucky from his arm into the blueberry sky over Prairieville. Mickey could see right away that the bird of prey scared away the doves and any other birds just by being in the same airspace.

From his chair, the binoculars followed Lucky testing the Prairieville winds by finding and kiting into the jetstream of air preferred by powerful birds with large wingspans. That made the old pilot smile. His arm became tired, so he leaned his elbow on his desk with the binoculars focused on Johnny. He started his glider and then launched it full throttle off the cliff line, joining Lucky in flight. Banking and rolling and swerving with the yellow bird, Lucky seemed to know in advance every command her handler was sending the glider by remote control radio signals.

They were flying at 120 feet, and Johnny knew that his eleven-pound glider could fly for twelve minutes on a full tank. He sent his glider up toward a large scudding cloud that was moving over Prairieville fast at perhaps a 1,100-foot ceiling that his glider could not reach.

The old pilot knew exactly what Johnny was doing. He was sending Lucky up into that massive cloud and using the glider to lead her there. Pond was thrilled to possibly witness something rare.

As the young pilot managed his controls, he explained to his new friend what he was doing. "Red-tailed hawks in courtship circle and soar to incredible heights. The male then dives down ... in a steep dive ... and shoots up again at nearly as steep an angle." As Johnny narrated and explained what he was doing, Mickey could see Lucky staying and circling at around four hundred feet. The yellow bird nosedived for a hundred feet, then climbed like a male hawk would do in a mating display. Johnny made his glider repeat this maneuver several times until Lucky was within a two-hundred-foot ceiling of the cloud cover. Running low on fuel Johnny explained, "I have to get the plane above Lucky and approach her from above," which the pilot did as Pond and Mickey admired how close he got his glider to Lucky at such a high altitude. "The male will extend his legs ... and touch or grasp the female briefly. Then ... they grab onto one another ... and interlock talons."

Incredibly, Lucky latched her talons onto the plane's fuselage, and they began a spiraling nosedive toward the earth at a steep angle. At three hundred feet, Lucky released her grip and freed herself from the perilous courtship dance she had performed instinctively. Both boys and the old man were thrilled over what they had just witnessed.

"Sweet!" Mickey had yelled several times during the aviary stunt.

It was the old pilot, Wallis Pond, who knew how truly incredible it was. Johnny circled and landed his glider onto a straight stretch of blacktop and stopped it on a dime in front of the closed sliding door of the barn.

The excitement of seeing Lucky's mating dive with the glider had made Wallis clutch at his weak heart and pop in a blue heart pill from one of the many vials in his pockets. He waited for his fluttering heart to slow before donning his black leather slippers he always wore around the house. He was going outside to congratulate his handyman's son. Wallis had decided several months ago to fund the boy's aviation school tuition at the Marshall Airfield twenty miles north of Kenwick. He put on his dark prescription sunglasses and a faded red T-shirt. Inside his shirt pocket he stashed another blue pill — just in case.

Johnny let Lucky soar above Prairieville until he and Mickey reached the green wagon. Then he kissed the air for Lucky to come land on her perch. Mickey watched the hawk respond without delay until she landed gently on the moving perch as they headed for the glider in front of the barn door.

Mickey's heart began to flutter when he saw the old man in dark shades leaving his front door and steering his chair down his ramp. He was wearing a beige Panama hat that covered his pale head.

"Well ... looks like you're gonna meet your dad real soon, Mickey Ditwell," Johnny teased while stopping to give Lucky a few seeds and a capful of cold water from the bottle in the wagon.

Poor Mickey was into his head, his eyes fixed on the old man's chair that buzzed toward them until it stopped beside the glider. Mickey's heart was beating as fast as Lucky's. They were now within fifty yards of the famous Wallis Pond.

"I want you to introduce me as Mickey Ditwell. Will you do that, Johnny?"

He'd asked the question with such seriousness that all Johnny could say was, "Yeah ... sure ... Mickey Ditwell." Then Johnny added, "Remember ... he's got a weak heart."

"That makes two of us."

"Johnny soon called out to their host, "You catch that mating dive, Mr. P?"

The old man smiled and waved his approval of what he'd seen with his binoculars. Mickey's mind raced with things he should and shouldn't say to his father whom he was meeting for the first time in his life.

"You ready for aviation school with Wade Hampton?" the old man grinned. He then reached for the blue pill fast upon seeing the boy he somehow knew was his son. A micro-flash of thoughts flew through his mind before the pill was swallowed down his wrinkled throat. He saw himself when he was tramping out West, living on the road at eighteen. So many scenes moved across his memory, yet he caught each one as his eyes remained on the boy in black. It was the summer of 1950 in Missoula, Montana. Eighteen-year-old Wallis was passing through a place he had visited many times, and now he was but a few months away from publishing his first book. He was headed for Dakota Falls on a tip that a printing company there was willing to work with and print books for new self-published writers.

44

Young Wallis also wore black then. He was tall and lean like the boy standing beside Johnny, looking down at Lucky as if waiting for Johnny's introduction.

"Mr. P ... this is Mickey Ditwell ... from Madisonville."

Mickey walked up to the old man and shook his hand, saying, "Pleased to meet you, sir."

"Welcome to Prairieville, Mickey," he smiled up at the boy who had his gray eyes and his mother's brindle-colored hair that he could see just below the boy's black baseball cap. "That was quite a show, Mr. Apple. How'd you get her to grip that glider, is what I'd like to know."

"I didn't. She just did it," Johnny answered with confidence. "Mr. P, can I show Mickey Superland?"

"Sure!"

Johnny slid open the barn door and they all went inside the cool, dark barn that smelled of gasoline, old tires, and paint fumes. Wallis Pond zoomed ahead of them and parked facing the most treasured thing he owned.

To Begin ... Again

It had been clear to Eddie for a long time. Returning home to his family, then working in the family bar, then driving a cab for several years had caused him to settle into a comfort zone of discontent — a false anodyne that had diminished his present-moment awareness he'd found when he had "awakened" beside that lake in Oklahoma.

A move like this had to be made in order to recapture the enlightened, luminous glow of awareness that was so important to him. His father was dead, and now his mother was settled into an assisted living facility near his sister, Sara, and her happy family in Lincoln, Nebraska. Their mobile home and his cab were sold. Everything he owned was rolling with him in his mother's '96 Olds, a gift she had signed over to him when he sold his cab.

He could hardly believe he was cruising up Interstate 29 and closing in on the Woodbury exit, which would take him into southwest Minnesota and to the home of his favorite author. *I should have done this years ago ...* He stopped his recriminating thought by reminding himself, *only "now" is real ... and nothing real can be threatened.*

Yes, Eddie was traveling as light as his uncluttered mind, with no past to dwell on and a future he'd taught himself to kill by staying in the present. It had been several years since he wrote his only novel, *Blue River,* and finished his grueling venture to sell out his two printings of five thousand copies each.

Eddie hadn't heard back from Mr. Pond since he wrote him that he was coming to visit him. But he wasn't too concerned because he had written in his letter that he had to clear up some family business first and would arrive as soon as he was finished.

Driving north on Highway 75, he was close to Lemon, Iowa, "the ice cream capital of the world." It was home to the Lemon Ice Cream empire, the company Karl Spink was forced to retire from early when his wife Marilyn left him.

Several Wallis Pond graduates came from Lemon. Eddie knew from reading all of the titles in the Wallis Pond series that Pond's leading character, Billy Lake, had learned how to cut and style women's hair in one of the small beauty shops in Lemon. Young Billy would drift from town to town looking for work — and love. He met all kinds of women who worked in towns like Lemon. But Pond's readers always knew that Billy was looking for the right woman to replace his mother. He would seduce her, then leave her just as his mother had left him alone in the world when he was just a boy.

Just like Eddie Dense, thousands of loyal readers were waiting for Wallis Pond's last book. In his last published title, Billy was closing in on the day he finally found his mother.

Eddie had been honest with himself about this trip to Prairieville. Pond's generous offer of two hundred thousand dollars for Eddie's help in writing and marketing his last book to all of his loyal readers was indeed a factor in deciding to finally make this trip. The ex-cab-driver had managed to save thirty-seven thousand dollars driving cab, plus another three thousand from the sale of his cab gave him forty thousand dollars in the bank. Eddie wasn't desperate for money; but with the cost of assisted living, he knew what he had saved may not last long.

Leaving the northern outskirt of Lemon in the pollen-drenched ether of August, the flat, two-lane blacktop road stretched north through the heart of Dutch farm country. Eddie recalled the letter he had written to himself on his last night driving a cab. As he sat under his dome light, his thoughts transferred from him, through the pen, and onto paper:

The real me was not in my book, Blue River. *I was not even "here" when I wrote the damn thing. Now I have quieted my mind long enough to know that this move is my "frozen moment" — that time in a man's life when he must sink or swim in the miasmic manswarm and live the way he truly wants to live. I must fly out of my warm nest and take this offer, perhaps writing about my experiences along the way, instead of only observing life from a cab ... talking to unconscious reflections in a mirror ... rushing back and forth over the same roads to shuttle the same faces to their predictable destinations. To begin ... again.*

Eddie had stayed in Council Bluffs for his family. Unlike his youth, he wasn't the kind of man to just hit the road and live his life. His sister was busy raising her new family, so his mother would have been left alone after his father died.

But now things were different. And "different' was another reason he wrote the letter to Wallis Pond. At forty years of age, and having read all of the Billy Lake chronicles, Eddie began to see common denominators between himself and the lifelong bachelor Wallis Pond. They were both writers and reclusive in similar ways. Eddie recalled a passage from one of Wallis Pond's later novels:

I doubt I will ever marry and know I will never raise a child. I don't know how I could. Husbands and fathers are important things and deserve most of a man's time to do them well. My books are my children and my readers my lovers. I will be loyal to all of them until my ashes are scattered over Prairieville.

As he approached the Minnesota border, Eddie was excited at the prospect of meeting his favorite writer. Nothing now bothered Eddie's quiet mind. He was free to see the rural farmland of northwest Iowa for the first time on his trip, and he was now ready to accept whatever happened on this move. To Eddie, it was a divine, perfect destiny. Just as his mind was debt free, he had created a life that many would envy. Only his mother and sister would care about his second effort to market another book. Eddie had no close friends who would miss him. He was alone — as Wallis Pond had been all his life.

At a roadside parking area north of Sibley, Iowa, Eddie pulled in and retrieved from his newly purchased leather briefcase the copied pages of one of Pond's earlier published titles. In awe of how young Wallis began his life, Eddie had read the titled chapter "Go Find Your Father" at least a dozen times. Under the shade of a tree with the windows rolled down, Eddie read it again.

As a boy, I taught myself to read and write in that black-and-white era of the late 1930s. I was riding the rails of the American West like a hobo. It was not at all a bad way to grow up. Most folks were poor in those days. And so was I, William "Billy" Lake.

Edna Lake, my mother, was a gypsy hairdresser who had moved by train from town to town in the Midwest before she had me. However, she still moved on while carrying me and after delivering me, her only child.

My mother at thirty years of age was a strikingly beautiful woman with a serious demeanor that intimidated both men and women. But not Alvin Lake, my father.

My father was in his forties when he walked confidently into Betty's Hair Boutique in Madison, Wisconsin, in need of a haircut and shave. Of course, my mother, Edna, was the stylist who would clean up Alvin Lake — in many ways that he paid for. My mother had told me that from the moment she shampooed and cut his brindle-colored, unkempt hair, and all the way through his close shave, he kept his eyes shut and didn't say a word.

During her work on this walk-in client, she began to see that he was transforming into a man she was becoming more and more attracted to and intrigued by. Months later she would tell my future father, "It was as if you needed me to teach you a thing or two that would make you grow up and become a man."

Poor Alvin Lake. The itinerant, womanizing drifter soon found himself willing to settle down and become a faithful husband and provider for my mother and me. However, my iron-willed mother told my father that she would never remain married to a man "just because he knocked me up." So after the first year of my life, my mother ordered my father to "hit the road ... and take your son with you!"

Since Edna was such a dead-serious woman, she scared my father. He hit the road without me and without a word to my hard-headed mother.

One late spring night six years later — at the ripe, old age of seven — my mother and I got off the train in Peoria, Illinois. I was following behind her and dragging one of her huge suitcases across the platform. As had been the case for as long as I could remember, we were on our way to another town, another salon in her circuit of respected salons across the Midwest.

But this time was different. She put fifty dollars in my little hand and told me to "get back on that train ... and go find your father." That was it. She gave me one of her expensive silk clothing bags and told me to put all my clothes in it.

I started crying, begging her to let me stay with her as I nearly filled that red bag with all of my clothes. She couldn't have been more unmoved and aloof, standing there so indifferently in the mink hat and mink shoulder stole she had purchased wholesale from one of her "salon connections." All the while, she was smoking her cigarette with that black ivory filter tip given to her by one of her "connections."

I can still see her smoking so carefully, not wanting to get any ashes or drifting smoke on her expensive brown wool traveling suit or her two-hundred-dollar brown, leather-laced ankle shoes. One thing my mother did have was shoes. I remember those empirical shoes tapping so impatiently yet so oblivious to my plight. She was like some spoiled sybarite who had to unload her whimpering baggage in order to be free and get on with her life. It was all so cruel and horrible — and so vividly remembered in detail.

Edna Lake never looked back at me. It didn't even occur to her to make sure I was seated safely behind one *of the train's coach windows. I doubt if she even heard the Burlington coaches squealing away from the depot.*

But I could see her. I stared at her, knowing in my trembling heart as my window seat passed her that I'd never see her again. She was not at all affected by sending me away. I could see her walking away from the boarding area. A Negro baggage porter followed her, pushing her baggage topped by her hat boxes on his cart.

Those awful words rang in my ears. "Go find your father!" They still ring in my ears today as a siren of fear. The night before she sent me on my way, she had said those same words. "It's time for you to go find your father. I can't be dragging a kid with me. I have to be free to move from job to job whenever I feel like it. You should be with your father now. It's his turn to babysit you."

After transferring my clothes to the smaller silk bag, my mother pulled a color-faded postcard from inside her purse and handed it to me. It was the last she'd heard from my father some two years prior. The postcard was a colored photo of downtown Missoula, Montana, and its surrounding golden hills. The Clark Fork River snaked through the Bitterroot Valley in the background. Missoula looked like an Old West town with saloons, horse-pulled buggies, and Model Ts parked on Main Street. She then handed me a one-way ticket to Missoula and told me I'd likely find my father in one of those saloons.

The train moved past the flickering gas lamps of Peoria into the inky blackness of the country. "Go find your father" scared me more than ever as I sliced into the darkness, beginning my 1,500-mile train ride.

I neatly folded the postcard and placed it inside my front trouser pocket. I often removed it from my pocket and looked at it, not knowing at the time how far I had to go before reaching the place where my father could be.

That first night on the train as I crossed the Mississippi River into the rolling mounds of eastern Iowa was the longest of my life. The clackity-clack of the wheels on the tracks made it seem as if I was riding a cauldron of death to the very depths of hell. I knew I'd somehow have to learn to talk to strangers — those people of different shapes and sizes with their sweet or offensive smells that often made me gag for air.

I had periods of solitude to cry in the throes of my aloneness on that train. My fitful sleep had me waking up frequently among the sleeping snores of passengers. Sometime in the middle of the night I got up from my window seat and stood under a gas lamp burning at one end of the rumbling coach. The light made me feel better. Then I removed the only photo I had of my father that I kept safely stowed inside the breast pocket of my gray wool jacket.

Inside my frightened head I would practice showing the photo to strangers. It was a black-and-white photo of a tall, slim man standing against a wall in his worn black suit and fedora hat pushed back and angled so carefree on his handsome head. He appeared to be a man who didn't make mistakes. There was a toothpick raised at the corner of his mouth by his grin. My mother had taken the photo outside a Madison, Wisconsin, restaurant not long after they first met.

Does he look the same? *I wondered under the flickering light. From where I stood, I could see the sleeping passengers, their vibrating heads resting on pillows on their reclined seats. They were covered with coats and blankets up to their necks and darkened by the blackness of farmed land at night. Their bodies shook in unison from the ride over steel rails that made the ceaseless sound of grind and squeal of steel on steel.*

Kindness from strangers over that six-day train ride made me realize that the world away from my mother wasn't so bad after all. What really hit me — straight into my young heart — was that I had always been on my own, fending for myself in a thousand ways, moving to a different hotel every three months with a mother who really loathed and resented me. She said I reminded her of my "worthless" father.

Watching the men on the train play card games, I soon learned not to gamble because I knew right away I had no way of replacing my losses. The more I forced myself to meet people, the more fun I had and the faster went the long train ride.

I stepped off the train at Missoula's Burlington Northern depot one morning and found myself smack-dab in the middle of the Old West. Rough and weathered men and women in cowboy boots and hats were everywhere. The town and people in it looked like a page out of the history books my mother checked out for me in the Midwest libraries.

In Missoula's whirling display of time-gone-by, I scoped every man's face with the eyes of a frightened boy, hoping to find the same man pressed against my fast-beating heart — the man who would surely be happy to see me and want to take care of me.

Downtown Missoula was loaded with dozens of dive bars where Alvin Lake was certain to frequent if he were still in town. Those dark, smoke-filled places were crowded with rheumy-eyed gamblers playing cards at tables. Tough, leather-faced, lean men of all ages were drinking beer and hard whiskey on barstools.

Bar after bar, the same scenario played out. Slowly I'd walk from man to man, my photo clenched in both hands and looking at each stranger quick-like. After scrutinizing each face in the bar, I'd stand at the end of the bar until the bartender came over to me. I'd show him my father's picture, and usually the bartender recognized the face, saying he'd seen him before. But none ever had a recent recollection of seeing Alvin Lake.

I scoured the whole town, showing his photo to scores of people every day and every night in all kinds *of scary places. Beside the Clark Fork River at night, I'd show his picture to drifters and indigents huddled around fires and drinking whiskey from bottles passed from person to person. As the nights wore on, I would always have to get away from the fire's comfort and retreat into the cold darkness before one or more of the drunken men would press me for money.*

I never did find my father in Missoula. I stayed the entire summer, sleeping in alleys in hiding places and scrounging for food. By the end of the summer, the money my mother gave me was nearly gone. About the time the nights became freezing cold in early fall and the soles of my shoes were flapping loud with every step, I headed west after sneaking onto a boxcar at the depot where I'd arrived some four months earlier.

I rode the rails all the way to the golden hills of northern California, often sustained by a shared can of beans or scraps of bread provided by some drifters I trusted. Never once did I fail to show my father's worn photo to anyone I met. And never once had anyone known or remembered Alvin Lake.

At the ripe old age of ten, I had become a streetwise survivor. That's when I stopped ducking into alleyway hiding places for safety and started walking confidently into public libraries. I began reading books and eventually improved my reading and writing skills. Little did I know at the time, that would be the foundation of what would eventually be the driving force of my life — writing and selling my books to others who could learn from my trials.

For the next decade, I kept the same old photo of my father in my breast pocket and still scanned every face I encountered in a seemingly endless mission to find my father. Over thousands and thousands of miles I showed his likeness to anyone I met on rails, roads, under bridges, beside countless lakes and rivers, in ten thousand bars and cafés, at thousands of campsites, and

54

at every possible place where lost men gather to keep from being alone.

There it was! His black vintage 1927 Monocoupe 70 with "Superland" printed in large, cursive, orange-colored lettering along the plane's fuselage was parked to the back of the barn. The boys had removed the canvas tarp covering the plane to reveal an antiquated piece of history that few in the 21st century would ever have the privilege of seeing. Wallis Pond told Johnny to turn on the stringed light above the plane he'd learned to fly in his early twenties.

The old pilot let the boys have a turn climbing into the cockpit. When Mickey lowered himself into the seat, he let out a quiet but enthusiastic "Sweeeet," which made Pond giggle and interlock his massive, arthritic hands into a ball of purple veins and old bones.

The old aviator enjoyed telling the boys how this model was the most popular high-performance small plane in its day. "Charles Lindbergh owned one exactly like this one ... and he could fly anything he wanted!"

They inspected the plane's thin, red-rimmed landing wheels that looked like they belonged on a soapbox derby entry. Johnny proudly informed Mickey, "Superland is a V-braced, high-winged, reliable radial-engine plane that's nearly twenty feet long, has a thirty-foot wingspan, and a cruising speed of one hundred miles per hour."

"He's a cool guy," Johnny said to Mickey as the two stood by his wagon. Wallis Pond had gone inside the house to make some lemonade for his visitors. "I thought that went pretty well after I told him your name," Johnny said. He gave Lucky some seeds and water before dismantling the wings of his plane and putting it inside his wagon.

"Sweet," Johnny agreed. "You could go to my school and graduate with me. It's K through twelve ... and there's not even thirty in my senior class."

"You have your clothes and stuff in the car?" Pond asked his son.

"Yes, sir."

Pond folded his big hands on the table and gave his orders. "Mickey ... bring your car here. Park it in front so you can use the front door to haul in your things and shoot them right up the stairs," he pointed. Then as he speed-dialed Johnny's father and put the phone up to his ear he said to Johnny, "I'll have your dad drive the car back to the farm and you can follow him in my truck."

"Okay," Johnny nodded while reaching for another protein bar.

Lloyd Apple answered his phone right away — as he always did whenever his boss called him "at his office" on a barstool at the Kenwick Tavern. The boys listened and chewed like hungry squirrels. "I need you to drive a car to Madisonville, South Dakota. You can pick up the car here in an hour. Your son will follow you in the truck ... Okay."

That was it. One phone call and Mickey Ditwell was free. Free of Ned and Bert and that boring farm in the sticks.

Before they left to walk back to the Spink house, Mickey noticed a reflection of a rainbow prism on the white refrigerator. It was coming from a plastic rainbow hanging inconspicuously on the kitchen window where sunlight was hitting it just right between the slatted curtains. The rainbow was a sign to Mickey that he was in a good space to create his music.

The fifteen-minute walk to Ned's car was filled with excited plans and great hope for the future.

* * * * *

Katie was thrilled to meet her half-brother, and mild-mannered Karl liked the boy right away. With the help of Karl, Katie and Johnny, the move into Prairieville was fast. It took each person only two trips up the mahogany stairs to get Mickey completely moved in.

Since Wallis slept in the downstairs bedroom, Mickey got his host's furnished master bedroom with its huge full bath. The king-size bed had four posts of rich mahogany and was three times the size of the twin-size bed he had slept in on the farm.

Sweet, Mickey smiled to himself when he first laid eyes on his new room. He carefully stowed his new guitar and amp in the massive walk-in closet, and he hung the few clothes he had next to his father's vast winter wardrobe. There were many of the old man's memories stored in labeled boxes at the far end of the closet.

When they were all downstairs, short and stocky Lloyd Apple was at Pond's desk looking at directions to the Ditwell farm. Mickey had to show Lloyd on the map the best way to get to the farm from Madisonville.

Karl and Katie were dropped off at home by Johnny in Pond's old black truck. Lloyd drove the old truck most of the time and was permitted to keep it in his possession even when he was "off the clock." Johnny then followed his dad to the Ditwell farm. Wallis had given Lloyd a one-hundred-dollar bill and told him to fill both tanks, wanting to defuse Ned Ditwell as much as possible. Lloyd also carried a note his boss had dictated and told him to give the Ditwells: "Mr. and Mrs. Ditwell: My son will be living with me now, and I will handle all of his living expenses. Sincerely, Wallis Pond."

Alone with his father for the first time, Mickey stared at the huge blackened fireplace in the main room that Lloyd kept supplied with kindling and firewood all winter. There was a big clock with Roman numerals on the mantel. As Wallis laboriously scribbled some notes to himself at his desk, Mickey could see a three-by-five card taped to his desk with highlighted, handwritten words that quoted Tennessee Williams: "Death is one moment ... and life is so many of them."

When Wallis backed his chair out and away from his desk, he saw Mickey browsing through the books in one of the many stacks of hardbacks piled against the wall. "I was going to have

Lloyd build me some low bookcases. But since I'm in this chair, they're so much easier for me to get at this way."

Mickey discovered a stack of paperback titles that were all written by Wallis Pond. "You wrote all these books?"

"Yes, I did," Pond chuckled.

"Do they have to be read in order?"

"Yep. The first book should be right on top."

Mickey picked up the title *Lost to the West*. "Mind if I read it?" he asked.

"Read anything you like. Anything in this house is fair game."

"Do you cook?" Mickey asked, curious how the old man handled his solitude.

"Not so well," Pond giggled, elated to have a roommate — especially his son. "How 'bout if I fix us some grub?"

"Sweet," Mickey smiled and followed Pond's moving chair into the kitchen. He watched his father prepare their meal, getting everything he needed from the drawers and cupboards below the countertop — another thing his caretaker had made accessible for his boss. "How long have you been in that wheelchair?"

"Too long," he chuckled. "I used a walker for as long as I could stand it. This thing moves along much faster than I ever could with that damn thing. I got so that if I sat down I couldn't get back up. So I stay in the chair."

After their meal, Mickey cleaned the dishes before Wallis gave him a tour of the first floor. In Pond's bedroom and bath, Lloyd installed overhead support bars so he could lift himself out of his chair. His full bath was widened and outfitted for wheelchair accessibility.

Near dusk, Mickey set out alone to walk the land of Prairieville — Wallis Pond's sanctuary from the hectic world that had made him a wealthy man. Behind the barn he headed down tall prairie grass ravines and gullies. They were alive with wind and flitting insects that made sounds Mickey was completely in tune with. Like his father, he was paying close attention to every detail surrounding him. Mickey's incredible sense of sound was a gift from his father, which Mickey would soon realize when reading *Lost to the West*.

He headed for trees surrounding a pond with a dock that Lloyd Apple had constructed. The water looked cool and inviting to Mickey, and he peeled off his clothes. Diving into the private oasis from the dock, the cool water felt good to his tired body after a very long day. He floated on his back and felt truly free for the first time in his life. As he stared up at the heavens, he watched the azure blue sky change by the minute as the sun sank below the horizon.

About the time Mickey was floating in his father's pond and ruminating on how perfectly his day had gone, Eddie Dense was leaving a café in LeRoy after a good meal and easy directions to Prairieville.

After many years, Eddie was going to finally meet Wallis Pond. This was bigger than the move he made when he left home to write his first book. And somehow he knew this move would tell him where he should live, where he should settle — as his favorite writer had done at Prairieville.

When Wallis went to his desk, he looked out the front window and watched a stranger's vehicle drive down his lane and park in front of his house. The orange hair of the driver instantly made the old writer think of the man who had published only one novel and who had written him the letter he cherished. As he watched Eddie Dense step out of his car, he resisted taking another blue pill for his excited heart..

The knock on the door startled his thoughts. "Come in!" he decided to bark from his desk with Eddie's open letter in front of him.

Upon entering the front door, Eddie could smell the books of a library. He smiled at his favorite author and said, "I'm Eddie Dense ... the writer."

Wallis smiled and extended his massive, palsied hand for Eddie to come and shake. "I see you found Prairieville," the elder author smiled.

"I got good directions at a café in LeRoy. This is quite a place you have." Eddie's blue eyes went outside to the cliff line. "Everything's just as you described it in your books."

Wallis could see the same light in Eddie's eyes that had once emanated from his own — aged eyes that were now cloudy and glazed by old pains and the medication to numb them.

"I've read every one of your books. I must say that Billy Lake's life always held my interest. I came here to learn how to live like that."

Pond only chuckled.

"You wrote so much about the ghosts of your parents haunting you and driving you to make something of yourself. I want that too. And I certainly want to read your 'last book.'"

Pond gave another chuckle and asked, "You want a cold beer?"

"That'd be great." Eddie followed the humming scooter into the kitchen. He popped a cold one and took a long drink.

"Today's been a great day," the old man volunteered. "I got to meet my son for the very first time today. In fact ... he's just moved in with me."

"I didn't know you had a son," Eddie said with a hint of surprise in his voice, but he was genuinely happy for the contented old man smiling up at him.

"It's a long story and it's all in my last book."

Eddie toasted Pond when the old man opened his beer, "To your new life with your son."

* * * * *

Marilyn Spink was livid after getting a call from Lloyd Apple's cell phone as he made his way west on I-90 toward the Ditwell farm. Lloyd was a double-agent who fed Marilyn information about his boss, mostly concerning his failing health. Marilyn promised to give Lloyd a piece of her inheritance from Pond's will and a lifelong job as caretaker of Prairieville as long as he kept her updated on Wallis Pond.

The only reason she had given Mickey permission to live with her during his senior year of high school was so that "this" didn't happen. Within ten minutes of getting her tip from Lloyd — even before the car had been returned to her parents — Marilyn was in her white Cadillac speeding toward Prairieville.

The mere fact that she and Wallis had a son made her think she would be left a hefty sum of money when Wallis died. And she knew Wallis Pond had nobody else in his life to leave his fortune to. Sure, there was Lloyd Apple, his caretaker. But he was a drunk, and she could easily manipulate him and buy his loyalty with little checks and a little flirting here and there. Mickey was not going to live with Wallis and threaten her inheritance. "Over my dead body," she swore to herself while heading east and closing in on the Minnesota state line.

Marilyn Spink had also made sure her daughter, Katie, didn't get too close to "the old codger" when she was living in Kenwick. She knew from Lloyd that most times when her daughter went to Prairieville, it was to watch Johnny fly his planes from the cliff line.

As Mickey was walking back from his swim in the pond, he saw the dreaded white Cadillac barreling down the lane toward him near the barn. *I ain't goin' with her,* he reminded himself as she parked next to a strange vehicle with Iowa license plates. Neither Marilyn nor Mickey had seen this other car before.

Marilyn started out nice. "What are you doing here?" she fake-smiled.

"I live here now, " Mickey answered with a confidence that threw her a bit.

"I thought it was agreed that you'd live with me and graduate in Dakota Falls."

"No ... I didn't agree to that. You were the one who said all that. I'm eighteen now and can live where I want."

"Why would you live here when he didn't want you all this time?" she said testily.

"Don't forget, you didn't want me either. He offered to let me live here. I decided to enroll in school here next week. I want to graduate here in Kenwick."

Her laugh made him blush, and the pimples near his mouth were cracking from talking after his swim.

"I just can't see it working out for you here. He's old and could die any day now," she said.

"I want to get to know my father. I'm going to read all his books."

"Oh ... really?"

"Yes. Really"

"Whose car is that?" she asked, changing the subject.

Mickey shrugged his shoulders.

Marilyn purposefully walked to the front door and entered without knocking with Mickey following but a few paces behind her. Wallis, in his chair, was showing books from his collection to the stranger with orange hair seated on the brown leather sofa. Marilyn, not caring about introductions, demanded an explanation from Wallis why he told Mickey he could live at Prairieville.

"Because he's my son ... and he wants to live here."

"I planned on having Mickey live with me."

"The boy's eighteen, Marilyn. He has no legal guardian. He can live where he wants."

Marilyn was upset and left the house without saying a word, slamming the front door on her way out. On her drive home, she knew she couldn't make Mickey live with her or avoid what may happen when the "old goat" kicked the bucket. *And who is that stranger with the orange hair? I suppose he's after the old man's money too!* Then she thought of the biggest threat to the inheritance: Pond himself. She knew he was capable of leaving her nothing and giving her share to some orphanage or crisis shelter.

She vowed to keep in touch with Lloyd about who was spending time with Wallis. That was all she could do — for now. It was important to her that Wallis didn't publish his last book. She knew him well enough to know that his final novel would be an exposé about their affair and would include details about the son both of them abandoned. Many of his loyal readers were trained and managed by her at the beauty college. She had always been discreet about her affair with the boss, even though everyone knew she was close to the boss.

She wondered if Lloyd could get the original manuscript or at least a copy for her to read. Marilyn pounded her steering wheel, knowing she'd have to wait to make contact with her spy. By this time he would be in the truck with his son, the boy she knew Wallis was fond of. Johnny Apple could be a real threat to everything she wanted — enough money to not have to live with a man. Marilyn Spink wanted her share.

* * * * *

Mickey helped Eddie move his clothes into the upstairs bedroom across the hall from his room. He liked Eddie right away. He knew he would be a good source for finding out things about his father since Eddie was a big fan of the Wallis Pond series.

Pond had offered to let the writer from Council Bluffs stay in his home in order to discuss marketing his last book to his loyal readers all over the Midwest.

It was Pond's idea to have Mickey play his music in the barn. Eddie went along with the young musician the next morning when Mickey carried his new guitar and amp to the barn to begin working on "LAT 44." He explained to his new roommate, "It's something I've been thinking about for years. I want to create my own music. They will be unique sounds never heard before ... and all mine."

Mickey plugged in his amp close to Lloyd Apple's workbench near Pond's neatly stowed tools. Eddie removed the tarp covering Superland to see the plane that carried Pond from town to town in his book-selling days and throughout many of his novels.

Mickey experimented intently with each string of his instrument, not at all interested in learning musical notes or chords. He paid close attention to the sounds made when he moved his left hand up and down the neck and picked each string to gauge the sound each move made, all while keeping the amp volumes as low as possible.

Eddie rubbed his hand over the surface of Superland. He saw the bent propeller and felt the dent on the nose from when Pond made his crash-landing at Prairieville. It had been the last time the experienced pilot ever flew in his life.

It was evident to Eddie that Mickey was serious about creating something with his guitar by the way he closed his eyes and truly listened to each mysterious note he played over and over. At times he picked the notes out rapidly, and other times he was slow and deliberate with his black pick that he was also getting a feel for.

Eddie leaned against the barn's open door listening for thirty minutes to Mickey's experimental beginnings. He stared at the purplish-pink rock of the cliff line across the way and recalled a passage from one of Pond's books where he talked about building his house at Prairieville:

Because of this seventy-foot-high cliff line's massive outcrop of rock known as Sioux quartzite, I knew that

67

my front window had to face it. I would build a house from the same rock and put my writing desk before a front-room window that faces the most majestic place in Prairieville.

When I was constructing the house, one of the Native American laborers told me he had heard stories about this land "where coyotes still howl." He said bison bones used to be piled in large quantities at the base of the cliff line. Then he pointed behind the old barn that was here and told me that a few hundred yards from here was a 1,200-foot-long line of rocks set in an east-west direction. Who built it and why is unknown, but it was well-known that on the first day of spring and the first day of fall, the sunrise and sunset are lined up perfectly on this rock line. This man also said that Prairieville was covered by a vast sea long before retreating glaciers buried the surface bedrock with a glacial drift of rock, sand and gravel two to three hundred feet deep.

And Prairieville has several places where cacti are found in Minnesota. Patches of prickly pear and brittle cacti can be found growing in the shallow soils atop the quartzite outcrop.

Eddie left the barn to explore Prairieville and identify some of the hundreds of different wildflowers and grasses growing on the property. He was especially interested in the bluestem prairie grasses that can grow up to seven feet tall and hide the grassland's sparrows, meadowlarks, nighthawks, and the stable population of red-tailed deer.

Behind the barn, still well within earshot of Mickey's testing of sound waves inside, Eddie could see that he knew this place better than he knew his own home — an ordinary mobile home park in Council Bluffs.

The pages of Pond's novel came alive before Eddie's eyes as he identified the plants the writer had described in vivid detail in his books. There were the yellows of the Missouri goldenrod and saw-toothed sunflower, the whites of milkweed and Queen Anne's lace, the blue-violets of purple prairie clover, and the red-pink of ironweed and thistle. *Yes,* Eddie said to himself while moving west into the tall grasses. *I need this land ... these colors ... to plant in me the drive to market another writer's book ... and to possibly begin my second novel.*

Then his present mind went back to the attractive woman that Pond said was Mickey's mother. Eddie knew she had to be in Pond's last book, and he was certain she had to play a major role in the old writer's life.

Advancing slowly over the vast prairie of grassland, Eddie knew that this had to be close to the spot where Superland crash-landed so many years ago. He continued on past the pond that Mickey had discovered and tasted with his bare flesh. Not far from the pond he knew there was a long stretch of hand-set rock running east and west. He surmised that ancient people must have used it to determine when to plant and harvest their crops.

Eddie had read that several times Pond turned down lucrative offers from university-funded geologist teams wanting to uncover artifacts from a lost civilization. Since Wallis paid a whopping $3.6 million just for the land of Prairieville, he didn't want a bunch of geologists digging up one inch of it. "Besides," he wrote, "if there are ancient burial grounds or bones of people under Prairieville soil, then they should be left alone — at least for as long as I'm alive."

Eddie noticed that Pond didn't have a formidable fence line and would discover that Prairieville was seldom encroached upon. The locals knew that Wallis Pond was a very wealthy man and a reclusive writer who cherished his solitude. There was no hunting allowed around Kenwick, so Prairieville was thriving and teeming with nature. As he made his way through the tall prairie grass, he came to a clearing. Beyond a ravine on the other side of a lush stand of black-eyed Susans was the mysterious line of rocks that stretched from east to west with a length of more than four football fields.

He made his way over to the three-foot-high rock formation and sat on it. He looked up to gauge the sun's path and could see that the yellow ball of August was just weeks away from fall's perfect alignment. *Why such a long path of rocks?* he wondered when looking east then west at the perfect line of ancient rocks. He watched the stilted, cautious steps of a great blue heron on its way to the pond.

Mickey turned up his amp and Eddie could hear his experimental notes. They were eerie sounds that rode the constant breezes blowing across Prairieville. As Eddie sat on the ancient rock formation, he realized that the novice musician was hitting a full scale of notes that suited this private sanctuary.

The night before, all three men stayed up late talking in the old man's front room about their plans for the future. Wallis asked Mickey about his life on the farm and what it was like to be home-schooled.

"I didn't like that part of my life," he had answered. "It was boring and made me anti-social. Now I'm ready to begin my new life," Mickey smiled at the two older men.

Eddie was impressed with the boy's answer and knew that Mickey Ditwell was truly the son of his favorite writer. He certainly had the potential to create something good.

Walking east through the tree line running the length of Kenwick Road, Eddie saw a girl with brindle-colored hair walking toward the house. She saw him sitting on the rocky sundial and waved to him. Eddie waved back and got up to follow her to the barn, where she would go listen to her brother's abstract music that she could hear riding the winds of Prairieville.

When Katie arrived at the barn, Mickey stopped playing. "Hey, sister Katie," he smiled.

"You're playing!"

"Yes! It's 'LAT 44.' That's the title. It's too early to tell ... but I can see that I'll get better."

"What's LAT 44 mean?" she asked, moving closer to her new-found brother.

"It's latitude 44 degrees, and Prairieville sits right on that airspace. I lived on lat. 44 on the farm too."

"Is there something special about it?"

"I hope so," Mickey answered seriously.

He played many different notes at different frequencies, with the volume up and down — a musical scale that had no musical tune remotely similar to anything Katie had heard before.

Eddie entered the barn and listened with Katie after he introduced himself. He could see she was a sweet girl in her teens. "You're Mickey's sister?"

"Half-sister," she smiled. "Are you a friend of Mr. P's?"

"Yeah ... and a big fan of his writing."

"You've read his books?"

"All of them ... except for one."

"Really? Which one?"

"His last one. He said I could read it."

"That's cool," Katie said.

"Have you read any of his books, Katie?"

"No ... But I will now that Mickey lives here. Mickey says he's going to read all his books too."

"Read what?" Mickey called out while stowing his guitar in its case.

"Mr. P's books!" Katie called back.

"Yeah ... He gave me his first book. I'll read them all ... in order."

"How's the music coming?" Eddie asked Mickey.

"Sweet. Real sweet."

The Lemon Man

Karl Spink was thirty-four when he met the twenty-three-year-old, dyed-blonde beauty Marilyn Ditwell at the annual Christmas bonus party for Lemon Ice Cream's salesmen. He looked older than his years in his silver-rimmed oval eyeglasses that were thick and magnified his blue eyes to the size of ping-pong balls.

Karl's lemon territory was the eastern half of South Dakota, including Dakota Falls — the biggest city in the state, and growing.

The bonus party was held in a popular Lemon, Iowa, steakhouse. Sharp-dressed Marilyn was there, invited by one of her students at Wallis Pond Beauty College, whose husband was also a salesman at the booming ice cream company. Yes, Marilyn was dressed to kill at the big feed-and-drink bash. And happy-go-lucky Karl Spink was her target when he received his record $4,200.00 Christmas bonus from old Walter Lemon. Old man Lemon was not only the president of the world's largest ice cream manufacturer and distributor, he was also the grandson of the founder of the town itself.

Poor Karl didn't really have a chance. She had been shopping for a husband. It had been over three years since she had delivered Mickey to her parents on the farm, and now she was wanting to start her life over. She was in the market for a "good man."

The ice cream salesmen, twenty-six in all, wore their winter lemon-colored jackets with matching pants and socks. All were envious of Karl — not only because of the attractive blonde from Dakota Falls who was obviously flirting with the perennial bachelor, but also for the new lemon-colored company SUV the sales rep had won for earning the highest yearly increase in gross sales.

After Walter Lemon gave Karl his bonus check and the keys to his new vehicle, Marilyn whispered to Karl at the table, "Perhaps I could get a ride home ... and be the first to ride in your new truck."

Poor Karl. He ended up spending the night in Marilyn's plush one-bedroom loft in downtown Dakota Falls — the same one Wallis had bought for her when they were dating.

As had been the case with Wallis, Marilyn got pregnant after only a few dates with the easygoing ice cream salesman. Every Friday Karl ended his week on the road by spending the weekend with Marilyn, bringing her half-gallons of several flavors of ice cream that Marilyn was consuming more and more during her first trimester.

Four months pregnant and they got hitched and honeymooned in northern Minnesota near the Canadian border. Karl bought a nice three-bedroom home in a new residential area on the eastern fringe of Lemon. The only thing behind their house was cornfields stretching for miles into the northwest Iowa horizon.

Katie Linn Spink was a daddy's girl right from the beginning of her life. She grew up fast into a freckle-faced, brindle-haired, blue-eyed little "Cutie Pie" — the name her doting father always called her. And Marilyn secretly resented the attention Katie got from Karl.

Since Marilyn was a high-maintenance shopper and was always depressed about her figure after giving birth to their daughter, Karl had to sell ice cream like gangbusters. He broke his personal best in sales year after year and won a new, lemon-colored SUV for nine straight years. Mild-mannered Karl Spink, the killer salesman of the Lemon Ice Cream Company, became known in the company as "The Lemon Man."

No man ever worked harder to keep and support a selfish woman in a life of luxury far beyond his annual salary of forty-two-thousand dollars than Karl. Although she retained her management position at Wallis Pond, Marilyn Spink was expensive. Often she'd leave Katie at daycare and drive to Dakota Falls to shop in the more expensive stores in the city. She'd buy new furniture for the entire house every three years.

They were on their third set of furniture when Marilyn started drinking alone at home and then driving to Dakota Falls or Woodbury late at night when Karl was on the road all week.

They slept in separate bedrooms for five of their last nine years of marriage. He knew she was seeing other men. Many times he'd see or find a suspicious business card of a man with his home telephone number scribbled in her handwriting. Hangups on the phone were frequent. And she never let him see the phone bill.

Thousands of times Karl looked the other way in denial and remained content to live for late Friday afternoons when he'd return home to his Cutie Pie. She'd always be waiting for him on their short, sloping front yard, anxiously and patiently anticipating having her daddy for the whole weekend. They would go to movies in Woodbury, twenty-five miles south of Lemon. Or they would spend hours just browsing in stores at the big Woodbury Mall after terrific meals in all kinds of restaurants that Marilyn hated. They were all alone and together. Every weekend. Always.

Katie called her reunions on Friday with her daddy "Good Friday." Marilyn called it the same because Karl would be her free sitter on weekends instead of that expensive daycare in Lemon.

Marilyn would change her hair color about every other week at Wallis Pond, and she continued shopping and charging things left and right on poor Karl's credit cards. And her job was in real jeopardy ever since Wallis found out she was running around Dakota Falls with other men — mostly wealthy married men. Wallis hired a private detective to follow his manager and report on her whereabouts to the concerned beauty college proprietor. Oftentimes Marilyn was spending the night with the Cadman, whom Wallis knew and didn't like. Wallis liked Karl and knew he was a good man. Too good for the insecure Marilyn Ditwell Spink.

One summertime late afternoon on "Good Friday" when Katie was about to turn ten, Karl had enough blatant clues about his cheating wife to finally drive over to the Cadman's million-dollar home in Dakota Falls's most affluent neighborhood. Parked less than a block away from the Cadman's house in his lemon-colored SUV, he saw his wife's new white Cadillac parked in the car dealer's four-lane driveway — an obvious gift from the Cadman that she'd told Karl was a gift from Wallis.

Karl wasn't the kind of man to confront his wife on another man's turf. He made the sixty-five-mile drive home to Lemon where he knew his Cutie Pie would be expecting him.

Katie waited on the cool grass in front of her house. She had the movie picked out from the newspaper that she wanted to see that evening.

Frangible Karl, after leaving the Cadman's street, was in no mood to see the love story his daughter was looking forward to seeing. Upon parking in the Spink driveway he told Katie, "No movie tonight, Cutie Pie ... I don't feel so good."

That night while Katie watched television in the living room, her dad was hitting the liquor cabinet like a sailor on a two-day leave. She saw him go to bed early — about nine o-clock — and she went to bed herself at ten with her mother still missing in action.

Later that night Katie was awakened by the awful noise of her mother yelling at her father in the master bathroom. They were ugly words about how "worthless" and "weak" he was. Katie made a child's mistake of getting out of bed to investigate the source of the ruckus, only to see the horrible sight of her daddy sickly drunk on his knees vomiting into the toilet.

Marilyn didn't bother shielding their daughter from the terrible sight. "Just look at your father! See how worthless and pitiful he looks now! And remember this when you wonder why I have to get out of this house!"

Katie was so stunned to see her father's pathetic condition that she cried, pleading with her mother, "Help Daddy!"

But her mother would only call him awful names before leaving him alone in his misery, leading Katie away from the bathroom doorway before slamming the door shut.

That was the longest night of Katie's Spink's young life. That Sunday, ashamed and contrite, Karl took Katie to church where he cried for most of the service.

Not long after The Lemon Man's drunken episode, Marilyn Spink had her husband sell the house and move into the little beige house in Kenwick, which required storing most of their furnishings in a storage unit. She told Karl that she wanted to live near Wallis in his waning years because she felt that her invalid boss would leave her some money when he died. Her ultimatum to her meek husband was smart and final: "We move there or I divorce you and move there with Katie."

Within six months after their move to Kenwick, Marilyn had most of their "good furniture" and belongings moved to a storage unit in Dakota Falls that the Cadman owned. She left Karl and Katie to live with her rich boyfriend.

Wallis was so upset when he heard that she'd left Karl and was "shacking up" with the Cadman that he fired Marilyn and closed down his beauty college — for good. He had been contemplating closing Wallis Pond for several years, and his ex-floorwalker's infidelity made his decision for him.

Karl knew it was coming. The house in Kenwick was way too small and plain for Marilyn's style of living. Karl was forced to cash in his retirement savings of $160,000 at Lemon Ice Cream and take a part-time, twenty-hour-per-week job at the Kenwick Farmers Elevator in order to be home for Katie and raise her alone.

Katie reflected later how that awful night on a "Good Friday" had been a blessing in the long run. She loved living alone with her father and was glad her selfish mother was gone.

Mickey lay in bed wide awake, happy to be in his new home and already playing his music in his own space in the barn. He thought back to his first afternoon in Kenwick when he first met Katie and Karl. Johnny had formally introduced them on his return trip home with his wagon and then returned shortly to the Spink house to help with Mickey's move to Prairieville.

Karl's lemon-colored SUV was parked alongside Ned's car in the Spink driveway. Fourteen-year-old Katie came outside to see who the tall boy was who had parked in front of their house.

"Katie?" the boy asked.

"Yes," she answered a little tentatively, not knowing the stranger.

"I'm Mickey Ditwell ... from Madisonville ... your half-brother," he smiled and winced from cracking open a pimple near his mouth.

She turned his extended right hand into an exuberant hug with her five-foot-four-inch body and looked up to her tall brother. "What are you doing here?"

He could see that his sister had his mother's blue eyes, except these eyes smiled at him. "I live here now," he replied.

"Really!"

"Did you know that Mr. Pond is my dad?"

She nodded yes.

"Well ... I'm going to live with him."

"Really!"

"Yeah ... I just came from his house. We're gonna drive my stuff to his place, and I get to live upstairs."

"I can help you move your stuff in ... if ya want," Katie said enthusiastically.

"Sure! Johnny should be back soon. He's gonna drive my grandpa's car back to the farm."

Karl came outside and Katie introduced her brother to her dad. Karl had known about Mickey since he'd met Marilyn, and he was genuinely happy to finally meet the boy. Mickey felt good about Karl right away.

Mickey fell asleep in his comfortable king-size bed thinking about Katie and Karl and how he would have two more people in his life here that he really liked.

During Eddie's second night at Prairieville, he awoke before dawn having just dreamed about his imaginary son, Les Dense, who was in his novel *Blue River*. Mickey's likeness to Les was uncanny — their build, their age, and their affinity for music. From his second-story bedroom window, he could see the looming darkness of the cliff line below the full vanilla moon. Something from his dream he tried to recall. *Yes,* he remembered, *it was the way Mickey came into Pond's life when he was eighteen ... just as Les had come into my life in that dream I had in Oklahoma. And it has been eighteen years since I lost David and Jenna.*

It wasn't Eddie's mind trying to find comparisons to Mickey and Les. Rather, it was some kind of destiny of being — a way of seeing how he was related to all people who come into his life at any given time. "Now," he mumbled and smiled, reminding himself that nothing real can be threatened. Then he got back into bed to find more sleep.

The next Tuesday morning, Mickey rode his bike down Kenwick Road on his way to register for his senior year on the first day of school. Wallis had personally called Mrs. Flett, his son's home-school teacher in rural Madisonville, to have her fax her student's accreditations to the Kenwick K-12 principal in order for Mickey to be enrolled and start with the rest of the students.

He pedaled slowly, side-winding past the Spink house. He considered stopping, but he continued on and turned left on Main. On his right was the Kenwick Tavern, open at 8:00 a.m. for regulars. When he rode past the tavern, he happened to glance into the back parking lot and saw a white Cadillac parked near the bar's back door. He stopped and circled back, curious to see if it was his mother's car. It was. He saw the CADMAN license plate. From his point of view, he couldn't tell if anyone was behind the luxury car's tinted windows. As the Cadillac started up and slowly pulled out of the parking lot, Mickey moved quickly into a position where he was unseen by his mother inside the car, but he could see where the car was going.

He followed her, staying far enough behind her to not be detected by her, for three blocks. The Cadillac parked at the registration area of the Kenwick Motel on the northern edge of Kenwick. She got out of her car and entered the motel's office.

Mickey had ditched his bike in a patch of thick prairie grass, lying low with his bike and waiting and watching for his mother. Above the motel was a full moon, white and rare in daytime's azure-blue sky. Ned had called a moon like this a "farmer's moon," but for some inexplicable reason the old farmer never really explained why he gave it such a name.

Marilyn hurried back into her car and drove over to park in front of a motel room door at the very end of the ten-room row. Mickey saw a familiar man, Lloyd Apple, get out of her front passenger door and go into the room with her. He knew his mother was up to something devious, and he knew Johnny's dad was being used by her to get whatever she wanted.

He pedaled back toward Main where students were walking, driving, or being driven to school. Kenwick K-12 was an old, two-story, quartzite building that looked as solid as any school ever built. It had stood for over eighty years on the west side of this little town.

As he padlocked his Stingray to a bike rack near the front entrance, a familiar voice called out, "Hey, Mickey!" It was Johnny Apple. He was about fifty yards away and approaching him on foot, along with Karl and Katie.

Katie, dressed in gold-colored jeans and a navy-blue blouse, was excited to have her brother going to the same school. "Johnny's going to fly from the cliff line after school!" Katie saw that Mickey had his mind on something else, and she wondered why he was wearing the same black jeans and shirt he wore the first time she met him.

Karl hugged his daughter goodbye, wished them all a good day, and headed back down Main to his job at the elevator. For a moment Mickey felt sorry for Karl, watching him walking away in his green-and-white-checkered, short-sleeve shirt and gray work pants, toting his sack lunch, on his way to work. Mr. P had told Mickey and Eddie the night before about how Marilyn had taken half of Karl's retirement savings and cleaned out their joint checking account in the LeRoy State Bank before moving in with that "shyster car dealer" in Dakota Falls.

As they headed into the old school's front entrance, Mickey felt compassion for all of them — including himself. Now every one of them had an adverse connection to his mother's self-absorbed life.

Wallis handed Eddie a copy of *Superland,* his last book, that Mrs. Thistlethwaite had brought him that morning. He instructed Eddie not to let anyone else read his book and to return it to him when he was finished reading it. "I'm looking forward to your feedback, Mr. Dense. I value your opinion immensely."

"Is your offer to market *Superland* for two hundred thousand dollars still on the table?" Eddie asked.

"Yes, it is ... if you believe the book is marketable," the old author responded.

"Why so much? You told me you'd have ten thousand copies printed and sell them for twenty bucks a copy. That'll total two hundred thousand in gross sales ... leaving you with nothing for it."

"It's important to me that the damn thing is distributed to all of my loyal readers. They deserve to know the truth. Perhaps you will agree after reading it."

Eddie immediately went upstairs to his room to read the long-awaited title. He read it while propped up comfortably with pillows behind his upper back and his head close to the bedside lamp.

Mickey sat at a desk at the back of the twelfth-grade classroom and stared out the north-facing windows. Thirty seniors were in his graduating class. All day his mind was on Lloyd Apple, who he knew had slept with his mother by now in that motel room. He could never tell Johnny what he saw below that farmer's moon. Never.

Wallis Pond's first chapter in *Superland* was titled "Killing with Kindness." As was the case with so many of Pond's thousands of loyal readers, Eddie Dense was hoping this last title would at long last bring Billy Lake's quest to find his parents to an end. Eddie began reading slowly.

It was one of those cold and gray late-autumn days in Galena, Illinois — hometown of our gloomiest President, Ulysses S. Grant. He was called "Sam" when he lived there as a boy and into his early manhood.

I was eating in this historic hotel — a national landmark with its walls covered with old black-and-white photos from General Grant's visits. Sam Grant was more than famous in his hometown. He was the hero (with all his many faults) who forced Lee's surrender in the bloodiest war ever fought on American soil. In my opinion, the Civil War was so awful that Americans would never fight their own people again. And within hours, I would end my personal war with my mother.

One of the beauty shop owners in Galena told me that Edna Lake was living in an apartment behind the library on Sycamore Street. But the only way to get to Sycamore was to climb a four-story cement stairway some seventy-five feet high up a bluff. It was reminiscent of Vicksburg, Mississippi, the site of (in my opinion) Grant's greatest victory in the entire war. Photos I had just seen in the hotel's lobby showed Galena to be a mud-soaked, unpaved mire of roads and pathways.

After all the years of mostly searching for my father to no avail, I had no clue what I would say to her — the woman who had sent me away so long ago on that train that took me to Montana.

In the hotel's restaurant I drank a few beers to bolster my courage, which was out of character for me. The alcohol only made me dopey and angry. The fact that I was so successful now — wealthy — made no difference whatsoever. Again I was that scared boy who boarded that train all alone.

Outside the streets were empty for such a busy little tourist town as Galena. A short block away was a canal, and I decided to walk along it. This was the long way around to the more accessible end of Sycamore Street. I did not want to climb those stairs. I'd have to get my cane out of the rental car because I could not climb all those awful stairs without it. But I did not want her to see me with a cane. Most of you will understand that.

No wonder Grant was such a tenacious bulldog. He had to be to grow up on these damned hellish streets. My knees ached so bad that I had to stop and take four extra-strength Excedrin with only my saliva to wash them down.

My mind kept kicking the back of my tired eyeballs with visions of seeing her face — a face I'd imagined to be aged into ugliness.

Here I was with a booming business and thousands of loyal readers in a thousand places. Yet I was petrified to meet the old woman who could not have done anything close to the good things I had done with my life. I stood in front of her apartment building and looked at its manicured landscaping with its solid front security door that was locked. I thought about buying the old schoolhouse-converted-to-condos and booting her cold fanny to the street.

Under the glassed residential directly I saw her name, Edna Lake, and I removed from my wallet the old photo of my father I'd kept for all these years. I could not bring myself to buzz her apartment number beside her name. I heard the sound of a leaf blower coming from the back of the stately building and went toward it. A man turned off his machine in order to hear me after I'd waved and stood nearby.

"Thank you. My name is William Lake, and I'm looking for my mother. She lives here. Edna Lake."

"She's not here now. She's shopping. She took a cab awhile ago and should be back soon."

"Thank you. I'll wait."

The friendly man went back to his leaf blowing.

I waited in front of the three-story building for her cab to show. Apartment 301. It's just like her to live on the top floor so she can look down on everyone, *I thought to myself. After nearly an hour it started getting colder and windier, and pepper-sized snow pellets started falling. I would have to fly into those dark clouds when I took off in Superland from the Dubuque Airfield later that night.*

I tried to think of things to tell her and ask her — like if she knew anything about my father. I thought I would tell her how hard it was when she sent me away on that train in Peoria. But then I realized that what she had done had made me the financial success I am today. Then I thought I would tell her how rich I was and rub that in. It would feel good to at least give her the satisfaction of knowing that I had not become some wandering fool like my father.

Suddenly a wave of realization came over me that I had not trusted any woman enough to live a good and balanced life with her. All because of my mother. That's when I knew she had won. Oh, how I wished I was standing there with a beautiful wife who loved me! She would have love, compassion, trust and joy — all the things Edna Lake never showed me. And we would have happy children that Edna Lake would never know.

Then I thought about the son I had that nobody knew about. He must be around four years old. He wouldn't be much younger than I was when Edna first began plotting to dump me. I too had done the very same thing to my son that she had done to me. And I was really feeling that for the first time here in Galena.

I turned to the east to a splendid view that young Sam Grant must have known when Galena was a bustling river town. Sam's fame will live on here for thousands of years. History books tell of the remarkable compassion he had for his enemy. I wondered what Sam would say to me, but then I began to feel small and weak in comparison to the hardships he had to endure.

Yes, Sam, if you were here now, you would tell me, "Show compassion for Edna Lake because she delivered you into this world that you alone conquered. And now you stand here as a man who has been tested and made it this far — to see the glorious view that God has given you."

A white taxi approached the old building on Sycamore and slowed to a stop in front of it. I could make out the small figure of a gray-haired woman in the backseat of the cab. She was wearing one of her expensive hats. That's how I knew it was her. She still looked regal and proud and strong as she stepped onto the sidewalk while the driver got her grocery bags from the trunk.

I could feel my father's photo wet from my perspiring hand as she had not yet noticed me in her concern to get inside the building. "Excuse me ... are you Edna Lake?" I asked.

Those gray-blue eyes of my mother had softened some since I last saw her; however, she asked in her petulant way, "Who wants to know?"

I was taken aback by the snap in the husky voice that I knew was hers. "I'm Wallis ... your son."

She looked me over from head to toe to gauge what sort of fella I was. And to my surprise, she invited me

*inside. I grabbed a couple of grocery bags so the driver
didn't have to make two trips.*

*She was shorter than I remembered because her
upper body was now markedly hunched forward from
osteoporosis. In the elevator the tax driver commented
on the "bad weather." Her remarkable wit lashed back
at the driver, "The only bad weather is no weather."*

*The man only nodded submissively while holding
two bags of groceries to his chest. I could feel her eyes
looking me over in the elevator as if she was appraising
every piece of clothing, including my expensive Italian
leather shoes.*

*Inside her impressive apartment, I saw her tip her
driver five dollars. Since my knees were killing me from
my walk, I asked the man if he could pick me up in an
hour. Then I checked my watch to gauge the time.*

*"Yes, sir. I'll be out front in an hour." He also
checked his watch.*

"Thank you," I replied.

*I took a seat on one of her two plush velvet, high-
back armchairs while she made us hot tea and put away
her perishables. I could hear her hard heels clicking on
her kitchen's tile floor, then turn silent as she crossed
the beige carpet. She set down a silver tray with our
teacups, creamer and sugar dish, along with vanilla
wafers on a plate made of expensive china.*

*"This is a nice apartment. You have nice things," I
said.*

*My compliments didn't impress her. She only
shrugged upon sitting across from me on her matching
velvet loveseat and scoffed, "It'll outlive me."*

*We sipped our tea and I had no idea what to ask her,
except, "Did you stay in the salon business?"*

*"I had my own line of wigs and sold them to salons
for years," she answered matter-of-factly.*

*She asked me how I knew she lived there. I lied and
she caught me in it. I told her I didn't know for sure
where she lived. I knew she'd worked in Illinois and*

just happened to ask a salon owner in Galena if she knew an Edna Lake. Her stare was as cold as that night on the train depot platform. I looked away from her eyes, down to my cup of tea. As I picked it up I confessed, "Some time ago I found your Edna Lake Wig line on the Internet. Your ordering information had a Galena phone number ... and so I asked at a salon here if she knew where you lived.

The truth didn't mean much to her. I guess she felt that once she was lied to, she couldn't believe anything I said. I glanced at my watch. "All right ... I'll level with you. I've spent many years looking for my father. Do you know where he is ... or what became of him?"

The way she shook her head back and forth made me angry. And her words that came right after that were so bitter and meant to diminish me as if I were not a man who deserved her respect.

"Now, how would I know what became of that shiftless tramp? He didn't want to be a father or a husband. And I didn't want to be his wife or a mother to his child."

I couldn't respond.

She continued, "Did you expect me to be infirm or on my knees begging for your forgiveness? Well, I am NOT sorry for anything. Sorry is cancer. Call it guilt if you want. It's not for me. I was who I was before I met your father ... as I am today."

Her cavalier manner of superiority over me made my insides hotter than the black tea going down my throat. I realized that if I didn't leave soon, I could kill her — smack Mother Superior's wigged head with her silver tray. My hands and legs began quaking soon after my mind told me to end her miserable life. It bothered me that I couldn't keep my hand as steady as she could when I would lift her teacup to my lips. And those steely eyes saw it, and it tickled her to see that I was affected emotionally and she was not. It was a game to her — to not show compassion or feel love —

and yet she could sustain her health and not be wracked by disease.

Yet here I was, decades younger than her, and it was I who was unable to stand on my own without my cane for support. Because it was I who held onto anger until it lodged in my knees like a festering fever that would not leave me. How had she done it? But, then again, had she? What was that hump in her back? I had to ask her.

"How'd you get that hump in your back? What's it from?"

"Osteoporosis," she said.

"No ... what's it really from ... Edna Lake?"

"I don't know what you mean," she courtesy-smiled.

"I mean ... could your back be weighed down by the things you've done?"

"I don't hold onto that stuff," she said as she waved her manicured, wrinkled hand.

"Then what is the hump from? I mean ... you didn't spend your life hunched over a desk. So how did you get such a hump?"

"I told you already. Osteoporosis."

"Uh-huh," I forced a laugh from my angry throat.

"I've heard all about your so-called beauty college and that self-indulgent tripe you foist off to those stupid girls who read it."

"Have you read any of my books?"

"Of course not. Why would I read such drivel?"

"Well, if you had read them ... you would've read about a boy who became a man long before he should have. All because his mother sent him away to find his father. Does that sound familiar, Edna Lake?"

"And if you had found your father?" she coaxed me on while massaging her wrinkled neck with her manicured hand.

"What do you mean?" I asked.

"You really were invested in NOT finding him, it seems to me."

"How's that?"

"Well ... any two-bit private investigator for a few hundred dollars could have found him for you ... if you really wanted to find him. But that would mean that you would have to give up your identity as a poor, abandoned little boy." She sang the last three words in that demonic voice I despised.

She was right. My identity was wrapped up in my victimhood, and it didn't bother me to hear that. But there was something else she had managed to do with those words. I stopped hating her. I think it was because I accepted what she said as something that was true for me. That's when things changed.

"You know, Edna Lake ... you might've just helped me. Being here with you made me realize that I've been fueled by parents who tossed me away. It motivated me to prosper. So you and my father have given me the material world ... in a prosperous way."

"You did that for yourself," she pointed at me like I was guilty of a crime.

"Yes ... you are absolutely right. I chose to make money off you and my father. But I lost in other ways by not trusting anyone enough to have intimate relationships. Are you the same way? Do you have anyone in your life you are close to?"

She saw me looking around her immaculate living room for photos of loved ones that were not there. She didn't answer me, yet I had struck a nerve and sensed it.

I continued while feeling compassion for me and for her, "You won't find any pictures of people I love in my home either. I have my friend and editor ... and my loyal readers ... but nobody to share my life with who will miss me when I'm gone. I never married. Did you marry again after my father?"

"No," she answered in a voice that was faltering from her usual brusque confidence.

"Why didn't you try to stay in touch with me?" I asked her without a trace of emotion. While she *appeared to be choosing her words I added, "I did the same thing. I have a son that I didn't want ... and never tried to contact ... except I pay for his care. I was selfish and didn't want the responsibility or burden of raising a child. So I understand what you did. And in that way I am just like you and my father. Is that something I inherited?"*

She didn't answer me. Instead she elaborated about how she would go to the Children's Cancer Hospital in Chicago where she would personally make and fit her wigs for the children ... at no charge. She then brought out a photo album and showed me dozens of photos of smiling children wearing her wigs.

Time was flying by while I looked at each photo. I listened to this independent old woman crying as she recalled all their names and recited some of the heartbreaking things they had told her. I told her how much it meant to me to hear of this good work she did for those kids, and that I harbored no more resentment toward her for sending me away. She couldn't really show any regret or anything close to contrition, yet I was now able to get to my feet and tell her that I wished her well. I got downstairs just as my taxi was pulling up.

During the taxi ride to my rental car, I thought about how I left her apartment without attempting to hide from her the pain in my knees. Nothing had been said about staying in touch.

Some five months later, I went out of my way to go to Galena again. This time "Edna Lake" was not listed on the resident directory of her apartment building. I found out from another resident that she had died soon after I had visited her. "She had a pretty severe stroke and didn't last long after that," the longtime neighbor informed me.

I asked the nice old lady if anyone had come to handle her affairs after she died. There was nobody that she knew of.

It will be the same kind of aloneness when I die, except I will be different and leave most everything I own to my son. He will still know that I did not love him in the way that every boy needs a father to love him. Nonetheless, he will at least know that I thought of him ... in the only way I know how ... from a distance.

I pray that he will find people to love and can share his life with them. He will not have to worry about money, and he will be able to focus on a life he wants. It will be a new beginning for him. I hope he values the things I've left him because they'll enable him to be free to find value in relationships and things other than money.

Eddie stopped reading at the end of Pond's first chapter and stacked the read pages under the rest of the manuscript. He thought of Mickey Ditwell — and how lucky he was to be the son of Wallis Pond.

The first time Mickey saw Eddie meditating was the Saturday morning after his first full week in his new school. Mickey was returning to the house after his daily morning experimenting with LAT 44 behind the closed barn door.

He could see Eddie's relaxed silhouette facing the morning sun while seated at his father's desk. He waved at Eddie, but Eddie didn't wave back. Upon closer scrutiny, he could see that Eddie had his eyes closed. He decided to use the back door so as not to disturb Eddie.

After breakfast some forty minutes later, Mickey was surprised to see that Eddie's glowing face was still sitting there at the desk totally relaxed. Right then Mickey knew that meditation was something he needed and wanted to learn. His mother had told him about meditation; however, she talked about it more than she did it. But this guy, Eddie, was really doing it.

It wasn't long before Eddie got up and saw Mickey. Eddie was glad to show Mickey the art of meditation, and he gave his first lesson on the spot. He had Mickey sit in the same chair he had put at Pond's desk from the dining room set. He told Mickey to close his eyes and to breathe through his nose, following his entire breath. Then he told him to say to himself "breathe" when he inhaled, and to make sure his belly expanded out with each inhalation. "Then pause for a second ... and at the end of your exhalation," Eddie demonstrated, "say to yourself 'smile' as you slowly push out all of your air. And then smile," Eddie said with a grin.

Mickey took a few practice breaths.

"Good ... good. Now try to make the entire breath like a wave that extends from your hips and back ... and all the way up to your nose. You are breathing through three diaphragms." He pointed to each one on Mickey's body. "Pay attention to that little pause right after each inhalation and exhalation. And pay close attention to your thoughts ... how your mind wants to chatter. Now do this for ten minutes. I'll time ya. Ready ... go."

Eddie was amazed that Mickey was able to sit for three ten-minute sessions. Each session was good because Mickey noticed his mind's resistance to silence. Eddie told Mickey, "Most people have so many lightning-quick thoughts, they don't even notice them when they're having them."

Mickey was looking forward to increasing his time to fifteen minutes each night before bedtime and first thing in the morning. He admitted, "I need it for my music."

Eddie agreed, adding, "It's hard to do consistently ... because the mind will tell you you're bored. But if you don't pay attention to the subtle positive changes, you 'll drop it and immerse yourself in the material world. And that's nowhere."

"That's what my mom does. She may meditate, but then she goes straight for the material things she thinks will make her happy."

"What's your very first memory of your mother?" Eddie asked.

Mickey had no trouble recalling the rainy day his mother delivered him to the farm. "I was riding in the backseat ... alone ... and she was driving this big car. All my clothes were in this suitcase on the front seat. She was talking loud above the rain as she was driving ... but I was too young to know the words she was saying. I remember we left the city, and the next thing I knew was mud. So much mud and those awful smells of the farm when she carried me into that strange house."

"Do you remember how you felt at that time?"

"I was scared. Yet I was happy to get away from her. I think she was upset because I was glad to get away from her."

"It's amazing how both you and your father were pushed away by your mothers." Eddie had promised Mr. P that he wouldn't share what was written in *Superland,* so he thought it best that he talk to the old man first.

Soon Mickey was lying on the couch reading his father's first novel.

Later that day Eddie finished reading *Superland* and returned the copy to its author. They weren't able to discuss the story because Mickey was around the house. That's why Eddie was getting back into meditating. He wanted to discuss Pond's incredible last book with as much clarity as possible.

On Sunday Mr. P arranged for Lloyd Apple to drive Mickey to Dakota Falls where he could buy some new school clothes. Johnny would ride along in Mr. P's old truck.

Wallis wanted to be alone with Eddie when they discussed *Superland.* Eddie sat in a chair close to the author, who was in his motorized wheelchair with his manuscript in front of him on his desk. He asked the old man if he'd let Mickey read *Superland.*

"If he wants to," Wallis replied, looking tired for so early in the day.

"Since I've read all your books, I must say that it wrapped up Billy Lake's life to my liking."

Wallis was happy to hear that. He also wanted feedback on the details of "Billy's" last will and testament, which was in reality Wallis Pond's will that was already executed and filed with his attorney in Dakota Falls.

"I'm surprised you would even let your loyal readers know your will."

"Yes ... but as you know, *Superland* was written long before Mickey came into my life."

"Yes, I know. And in *Superland* you made clear your intentions to let your son know he did have a place in your life by leaving him everything. Does Johnny know you left your plane, Superland, to him?

"No."

"And Lloyd Apple and Marilyn, they don't know you left them out of your will?"

"No. They don't know anything about my will."

"There are many instances in the story where you know that Lloyd is working behind the scenes with Marilyn, yet all the while acting as your trusted caretaker."

"Yes. She's probably sleeping with him. In fact ... I'd bet on it."

"That is inferred in the story. Don't you think that would hurt Johnny and his mother?"

"Yes."

"And the things about Karl ... things Marilyn told you. Those things would hurt Karl and Katie."

"Yes. That's why I wanted to talk with you, Eddie. I don't think I should publish the book just now. Perhaps after I'm gone and after all three kids have read it. I will be paying for Johnny's flight school and Katie's college ... whether I publish the book or not. I want to offer you a proposition since you were led here by my offer to have you market my last book for two hundred thousand dollars."

"It would be understandable if you didn't publish *Superland*. I'm okay with it ... really, Mr. Pond."

"Now, hear me out. I would give you two hundred thousand dollars to stay on at Prairieville as the caretaker ... until Mickey is out of college or more mature and able to handle his inheritance."

"What about Lloyd Apple?"

"I don't want him here when I'm gone. I keep him employed for the sake of Johnny and his mother. And I keep him around so I know where he is. I don't want him or that conniving Marilyn at Prairieville for any reason when I'm gone. They'd only make trouble for Mickey," the old man said with obvious agitation.

"I can see that. So you may never publish *Superland?*"

"I want Mickey to read it ... later ... so he understands the whole scene around here. It might be his decision."

"I see."

Pond picked up the copy of *Superland* that Eddie read and steered his scooter over to his burning fireplace. He proceeded to burn the manuscript a few pages at a time while saying, "I want you to take the original manuscript there on my desk and hide it under the seat of Superland. There's a secret compartment on the floor that lifts up. You can put it in there until you feel Mickey is ready to read it.

Eddie placed the original manuscript inside a large envelope Pond gave him and headed for the barn. On his way to the barn his mind was going over Pond's incredible proposition.

Having stowed Pond's last book in the secret compartment in the antique plane, Eddie returned to the house to find Pond back at his desk. "So what are your thoughts about my offer?" he asked.

"Right now I'd have to say I can do it," Eddie replied.

"Good. I'll have my attorney set up everything ... with your good judgment deciding the end of your part of the bargain."

"That's fair," Eddie smiled.

He had Eddie write down his full name and Social Security number, along with Eddie's bank and account number in Council Bluffs. Then the old writer removed his reading glasses and said, "Mickey told me you taught him to meditate. That's when I knew you would be a good caretaker for him and Prairieville."

Eddie smiled and asked him if he planned on telling Mickey any of the things he'd written in his last book.

"I don't plan anything at my age," he chuckled.

After Lloyd dropped off the boys at the mall and told his son to call him when they were ready to go, he called Marilyn and informed her that her son was at the mall buying clothes. She told her informant to meet her at a bar they knew in ten minutes.

Lloyd was on his second beer when Marilyn arrived. They sat across from each other at a booth after she ordered a bloody Mary. "He's got this writer, Eddie from Council Bluffs, stayin' at the house. Mickey and the old man really like this guy," Lloyd said to the attractive divorcee.

"He's the guy that was there when I was a few weeks ago?"

"I guess. He's got orange hair."

"Yeah ... that's him," she said and took a sip from her glass. "Do you know why he's staying there?"

"Nope."

"Find out. And I want you to get me a copy of his last book. It should be around there somewhere."

"I don't know ... If he ever finds out I took his book ... he'll fire me for sure."

"If he knew you were sleeping with his son's mother ..." she smiled in her manipulative way. She opened her purse and handed Lloyd a new one-hundred-dollar bill, along with a threat: "If I don't get that book ... your wife won't like it."

"What's that s'posed to mean?"

"Think about it," she smiled.

"My wife has nothing to do with this," Lloyd said with such enmity that Marilyn knew she had reached Pond's caretaker.

"Just get me that book, Lloyd ... and you won't have to worry."

* * * * *

Maxine Gutierrez barely spoke English when Lloyd Apple met his soon-to-be Hispanic bride at her parents' Mexican restaurant in Marshall. The naive waitress was seventeen and Lloyd was thirty. Lloyd would pick her up after her shift and take her to movies in Marshall, then back to his modest house in Kenwick. She soon became pregnant with Johnny and ended up marrying Lloyd Apple.

Throughout her pregnancy, Maxine Apple took in ironing for extra money. Before long the interior of their two-bedroom home was adorned with clothes on hangers lined across makeshift clotheslines her husband had strung throughout the house. The Apple house always smelled like clean clothes and plastic from the sheer garment clothing bags she bought wholesale from a Hispanic dry cleaner in Marshall.

Tiny, frail Maxine Apple worked long and hard hours. The money she made helped supplement the family's income when Lloyd was fired from his good-paying job with the county as a garbage collector. Working for Wallis Pond earned Lloyd decent pay, but he didn't have any of the benefits he'd had with the county.

As baby Johnny grew, so did Maxine's business. Lloyd added on a closed deck that ran the entire length of the back of the Apple house. Maxine used the extra space to hang her clothes, which allowed her to expand her clientele to include LeRoy residents.

Maxine knew her husband was an alcoholic and that there was nothing she could do about it. She had her baby and her booming ironing business to keep her plenty busy. Her husband could stay away all day, and Maxine was fine with that. But he'd always return home for the evening meal, his own clothes saturated with the smells of the tavern and any jobs done at Prairieville.

Twelve- to sixteen-hour days were not uncommon for Maxine Apple. Lloyd had married a woman who would do more than her share to support her family — and without complaining along the way.

Eventually little Johnny discovered airplanes and outgrew the crowded house. The Apple backyard had enough airspace to toss his kit-made gliders from the branches of trees and then from the top of the tile-pitched roof of the one-stall garage.

It was Maxine who supported her son's love of flying by upgrading his fleet of planes to more expensive models that soon were buzzing all over Kenwick by remote control. When the boy pilot broke the neighbor's kitchen window by crashing one of his planes into it, Maxine had the window replaced without telling her husband anything about it. To Johnny's mother, flying seemed like a safe hobby for her only child compared to the violence of football that always repulsed her.

Sometimes she'd ride along to the Marshall Hobby Shop to make sure her son got everything he needed to continue his love of flying. Her husband would complain about the money she spent on Johnny's passion, but his words always fell on deaf ears. Maxine Apple was a giver. Lloyd was a taker. She would do anything she could to keep her son interested in his love for flying.

Never had Johnny's mother gone to the cliff line to watch him fly, but she would listen intently whenever he told her about a recent flight at Prairieville. As she listened, her boy's brown eyes would become animated when recalling the most minute details of his exhilarating flight in the precarious winds of Mr. P's Prairieville. When he was done talking, she would ask him the same question: "What do you do next?"

He would proceed to tell her about the new plane he wanted. Oftentimes he'd race to his room and bring her the picture of his next plane that he'd seen in the model airplane magazines that were free in the hobby stores.

Right away, Maxine would begin hounding her husband to take their son to Marshall so he could get what he wanted, reminding Lloyd, "You don't have to be a college graduate to fly airplanes for rich people or big companies."

Maxine Apple wanted her boy to be a pilot. And Johnny Apple wanted to be "the best aviator the world has ever known."

"Why you want such a thing?" she asked her boy in broken English.

"Because I was born to fly," he'd smile into her loving eyes.

Eddie recalled the last chapter of *Superland* he'd read. Billy Lake was an old man and dying. Wallis Pond put so much reality into his last book that Eddie dared call the manuscript Pond's memoirs. On the pages of his last chapter, "Bring Me a Mirror," he wrote in vivid detail:

I knew this had to be the last summer of my life. There were two special young people who lived in Kenwick. I wanted to do something for each of them while I was alive and able to see it.

For Johnny, I will pay for his flight school. If he is successfully licensed, I will leave him my Monocoupe 70, Superland, to fly when he is of legal age, twenty-one. I also flew Superland for the first time when I was twenty-one.

Katie is the other special young person. I was only able to see and talk with her on summer breaks when she and Johnny would clean for me in order to make a little spending money. Freckle-faced Katie would've been considered a "flapper" in my day for the independent and smart way she dresses herself. I know her mother well. And in spite of her mother, I gladly will have a trust fund put aside for her higher education.

These special young people came to visit me at the hospital when I had my first stroke. There I was, lying in that hospital bed, my head slightly elevated with plastic oxygen tubes inserted into my nostrils and an IV taped around a purple vein on top of my liver-spotted writing hand. They stepped up to my bed. When I opened my tired gray eyes I mumbled to them, "Bring me a mirror." They left my room upon searching to no avail for a mirror inside the bedside table drawer.

When they returned with an oval-shaped, handheld mirror from the nurses station, they put it up to my face. I smiled at the silver light emanating from my dying eyes.

They could see "my light" yet did not say anything. Both of those special young people could see that I was at peace after looking at my eyes.

Wallis Pond hadn't seen "his light" ever since he crash-landed at Prairieville, yet he always believed he'd see it again at the very end of his life. Pond wrote in many of his titles:

Beliefs make people inflexible and much too rigid to be open to any new ideas. Once I "believed" in something, I'd let it be in order to see if it would change over time. It usually did — only because I didn't own it or invest it as part of my identity, so I was able to let it go. If it wouldn't leave on its own, I would urge it to leave me. And it would.

Yet there was always this one belief that I held onto for most of my adult life: that there would be a light ahead of me when I'm close to death. If I could see this light coming out of my eyes, I would also be able to see it when my heart stopped.

I believe that if I want to come back to this world again in another body, I would turn away from the light and fear it. But not me. I would welcome the light and go to it. Because more than anything, I do not want to return or come back again to this world.

As Eddie ran his finger through the September dust on the hood of his car, he thought of the money Wallis Pond had deposited into his bank account and how he wasn't turning back. He would stay on at Prairieville and see if this place could become home.

Wallis's chair fit perfectly into Eddie's deep trunk, along with Johnny's dismantled glider and flying kit. It was the old man's idea for Johnny to fly at Palisades. Katie and Mickey would ride along with the rest of the group.

Palisades State Park and Wildlife Preserve was fifteen miles west of Prairieville, just across the border into South Dakota. Young Wallis would go there for overnight getaways and stay in one of the one-room cabins on the eastern bank of Split Rock Creek. At Palisades he could fish and write for hours on end.

They parked and unloaded the wheelchair from the trunk. In the scenic-view gazebo, they marveled at the jutting rose-colored quartzite that formed rock-ledge islands in the rushing rapids of the creek below them. In some places, the impressive creek was sixty feet wide. A 120-foot-long Pratt truss bridge spanned the water just off to the right of the gazebo. It was a century-old crossing fastened by sixteen-foot-wide wooden beams with diagonal braces to create a strong, rigid framework resting on natural abutments of Sioux quartzite.

Katie pointed to a family of mallards lounging in the large golden islands of tufted prairie grass that had fallen in lush strands along the creek's banks.

Eddie knew this beautiful oasis from Mr. P's books and asked, "So does this place bring back some memories for you?"

The old man chuckled, pointing further up the creek at the cabin he used to frequent. "I can't tell you every memory ... but, yes ... it does bring back many pleasant ones."

Eddie and Wallis watched Mickey and Katie help Johnny carry his plane and kit across the bridge. On the western bank of the creek, they turned south and headed for an open area that led up to the golden bluffs a hundred yards further west. Johnny launched his glider from the top of the bluff and once again thrilled Wallis Pond with his display of aerial acumen. For eleven minutes, the small yellow plane with blue trim danced in the autumn sky over Palisades. The sound of the buzzing glider drowned in the rushing waters before them.

Katie and Mickey had read Mr. P's first two novels. Both of them could see the old writer lost in his reverie — lost in the gray ghost of winds of years gone by when Wallis first came here as a young man.

It was shortly after he'd purchased Prairieville and had come to Palisades to write. Only Eddie had read *Superland* and learned about Dorothy Conklin from Mitchell, South Dakota. She was a graduate of Wallis Pond Beauty College who had recently opened her own beauty shop. Within a short time, it was a thriving business in the home of the Corn Palace. Dorothy was twenty-six and beautiful. She had raven-black hair that was long and suited her Native American heritage.

Dorothy had sent Wallis a birthday card and asked him what he was doing on his birthday. He called Dorothy and told her he was going to Palisades to write. On his birthday he arrived alone, checked into his cabin, and saw her standing on that old bridge. He wrote:

She had been watching me from the bridge. When I first saw her in that sheer cotton dress, standing barefoot and pointing one of her slender brown feet off the side of the bridge, I knew I would remember this birthday for as long as I lived.

When she waved I could see she was concealing a wrapped gift in her other hand behind her back. We walked toward each other, and my excitement grew knowing she had come from Mitchell on a surprise birthday visit.

We talked and cooked together on the deck of my cabin that faced the rushing creek waters and the setting sun in late May. I unwrapped the gift she brought me upon filling our first glass of red wine. After we toasted to my birthday, I tasted the wine again on her lips.

Her gift to me was a black leather writing folder that I would carry in Superland whenever I flew. I would never write about Dorothy until now, when I recall our two glorious days and nights as lovers at Palisades.

Dorothy was also a licensed massage therapist and was booked solid in her salon. I'd heard she was

getting a reputation as a "healer." She worked on my
sore back that was injured during my perilous landing
at Prairieville. Her hands were strong but gentle,
soothing bruised and tender muscles that responded to
her healing touch. The experience was made sensual by
coconut butter and lavender oil that warmed me all
over.

On the deck of the cabin, she talked about her large
family in Santee, Nebraska, and how they lived in abject
poverty on the reservation. There was no sense of
victimhood in her story, nor was there any emotional
need to explain or justify why she had never returned
home since graduating from the beauty college. I could
see clearly in those black and brown pools in her eyes
that she was not one for self-validation.

Our time together flew by as good times always do.
I never saw Dorothy again or communicated with her.
I'm not sure why two strangers can come together and
be such tender and caring lovers, then separate and
never return to each other. It happened to me at
Palisades in May when I was yet a young man.

They all enjoyed Johnny's performance of incredible banks, rolls, figure eights, and a series of flight maneuvers that seemed to impress the old pilot more than anyone else. Even other visitors at Palisades, including some rock climbers in the throes of scaling jutting quartzite, stopped to watch the aerial show of the yellow glider.

Once the aerial show had concluded and the three young people rejoined Eddie and Wallis, Johnny announced he had enrolled in flight school. The young pilot thanked Mr. P for paying for his tuition. On the bluff after landing his glider, he had told Mickey and Katie that when he enrolled, his flight instructor, Wade Hampton, informed him that his tuition was already paid in full by Wallis Pond.

Maxine Apple would have gladly paid for her son's flight school. The courses ran for sixteen weeks on Saturdays from ten in the morning until two in the afternoon. However, it was Lloyd who preferred to have his son wait until he graduated from high school. But Johnny didn't want to wait, and he told his father just that — and enrolled anyway.

While the kids explored Palisades after returning Johnny's glider and kit to Eddie's trunk, Eddie and Wallis headed north for the old cabin Wallis used to stay in. "I hope the cabin's open and vacant," Wallis said with palpable excitement. "I want to show you something I left in there."

Luckily the cabin was unlocked and vacant. Best of all, Wallis was able to drive his scooter right into the tiny place. From his chair he pointed down to the cabin's old oak floorboards. Eddie saw the initials "W.P." carved into the wood.

"W.P.," Eddie said.

"It's still there," Wallis chuckled. "I used my pocket knife to inscribe my initials there after having too much wine."

"Was that the birthday visit here with Dorothy?"

"Why, yes ... I believe it was," Wallis smiled, knowing Eddie had read about her in *Superland*.

"Was Dorothy her real name?"

"Heavens no! She might be married and would not appreciate that kind of stuff in an old man's novel."

"And yet you used Marilyn and Lloyd's real names ... and these kids."

"I don't give a crap what Lloyd and Marilyn think. They can both go to hell. But the kids ... I didn't think they'd mind ... after leaving them something."

"Johnny has to know his father's an alcoholic, but the spying he does for Marilyn in the book would make waves with both Johnny and his mother ... I would think."

"I know ... I know. The kids will know I did not want to hurt them in any way," Wallis stated with a certainty that Eddie agreed with.

"But can't Marilyn or Cadman or Lloyd sue your estate if *Superland* is published?"

"They could ... but they won't. They don't want that kind of publicity. Yet I think the kids should read the book to gauge their feelings about it. And I'll leave it up to Mickey whether he wants to publish the damn thing. Did you hear him play this morning?"

"Yes. He's improving."

"Oh, I should say he is!" Wallis slapped his thigh with his massive hand. "I listened to him outside the barn door. He's got some way of telling a story in his music. He's a true artist. I get lost in his spacings between notes ... not a clue what was coming next. And these notes would rise and fall like one of Johnny's gliders moving across the airspace. All three of those kids are artists. Katie makes her own clothes! Can you believe that? She made a scarf for me last Christmas ... a gray scarf. Just a month before Christmas she called me and asked me what my favorite color is."

"Anyone who reads your books knows that gray is your favorite color."

"Yes, I suppose they do," Wallis laughed.

"And because I've read all your books, I can tell you *why* gray is your favorite color. You said, 'Anyone who lives alone knows there is no blackness or whiteness to life. It's all gray ... the beautiful color gray.'"

Wallis giggled as they exited the cabin to collect the kids. They headed for the Dairy Queen in LeRoy. Mr. P was treating.

October in Kenwick was all so wonderful for Eddie. The air was flavored with the smells from smoking fireplaces and wood burners. This was the crispy, frosty season when oaks, maples, and elms are splashed with gold and red, orange and yellow. Verdant stripes of watermelon color were on every hedge and bush bordering and dividing the clean, modest homes of a working class of people mostly of German and Swedish heritage. Prairieville's blue spruce were fuller with a lush emerald color in bunched folds of branches juiced every morning by nature's frosty surfeit.

It was the romantic season for youth when boys Johnny and Mickey's age drive around after football games in LeRoy and Marshall and a hundred thousand other towns looking for boys they know and girls in high-neck sweaters they want to know. But Johnny Apple could be found in his garage experimenting with a mixture of five percent nitro methane and his regular fuel for extra engine power. Lucky, inside her large cage, would watch the boy for hours at a time. And Mickey Ditwell would be playing LAT 44 in the barn, experimenting with sound and the vibrations his body would feel when his guitar played notes at a certain pitch — sounds that he would meticulously memorize.

Then there was creative Katie, the third young artist Mr. P was so proud of. She had been sewing Halloween costumes like gangbusters for herself, her father, Mickey and Johnny for the party Mr. P agreed to have at Prairieville.

Wallis Pond was alive again. Even his private nurse, who came by every two weeks to check her patient's vitals, remarked how improved his blood pressure and pulse were in her last three visits. The old man dispatched Lloyd to a farmer's roadside stand in LeRoy to buy the biggest pumpkins he could get, along with sturdy candles to place inside them. Mickey and Johnny would carve them into jack-o-lanterns and place them on the edge of the cliff line Halloween night.

On his walk around Kenwick, Eddie stopped at the Spink house to see how Katie was coming along with the costumes. Instead of laboring at her sewing machine, she had been reading Pond's third novel and wanted to discuss the book with Eddie. "Mr. P hates America's materialism," Katie said. "Listen to what he wrote: 'The individual strivings of my own life were not isolated things. Rather, I was one ego-driven mind in a billion-footed herd of busy minds, each willfully pursuing their own selfish interests and desires.'"

"Yes," Eddie nodded. "He had a very different outlook on his career as a writer. He never was interested in being a nationwide, best-selling author because he believed he would be too far removed from his target audience. He developed a relatively small network of loyal readers throughout a five-state area. He wanted to maintain that one-on-one contact with his core group of readers so he would have a family of sorts without any of the emotional commitment. That's why he only wrote for them. He said after eight months of selling his books on the road he could then spend sixteen months writing his next book for his loyal readers without the stress of always gaining more — the materialism you mentioned. He also wrote that he was searching for an emotional balance but never found the right woman to give his life complete balance."

"That's so sad," Katie said.

"His health started going downhill soon after he crash-landed here and stopped flying. He had to reach his readers by car. Then when his knees got really bad, he had to use the mail without any one-on-one contact with his readers. He really missed that. In many towns he stayed in the homes of his readers. That's what kept him young. And now ... all he has is you, Mickey and Johnny."

"Yeah ... I guess. I'm anxious to read about Prairieville."

"That's what lured me here ... Prairieville," Eddie said reflectively.

* * * * *

At the front of Halloween night, before the temperature dropped considerably, Lloyd Apple drove his son to the party. Lloyd made fun of the gold-colored cape Katie made for Johnny to wear to the party, calling him a "fairy." But Johnny didn't care. He had recently aced his instrument exam in flight school and knew he soon would be flying for real with his instructor.

Johnny went with his dad to light a dozen jack-o-lanterns looming on the edge of the cliff line. Katie and Karl arrived and stood by their car gazing up at the illuminated orange pumpkins. The Spinks were dressed like gypsies in colorful loose pants and puffy shirts with bandanas. They laughed when they saw Johnny spreading his cape out while standing behind a pumpkin as if ready for flight from the cliff line.

Mickey stopped playing LAT 44 and came out of the barn in his costume of black leather pants and sleeveless black leather shirt with black wristbands on each wrist. He looked like a rock star with his red hammer tattoo and his brindle-colored hair greased back.

Mrs. Thistlethwaite and Pond's attorney were in the house talking to him at the dining room table. Maxine Apple was happily preparing the food and table for the catered party being thrown by her generous host.

Lloyd stood near Pond's old truck knowing Pond's attorney was in the house. Marilyn would love to know that, and he planned to call her and let her know the next morning.

Eddie came downstairs and helped Maxine set the table for the catered prime rib dinner the old man promised would be memorable.

Nine guests were seated at the dining table. Pond was in his chair at one end of the table, and Mrs. Thistlethwaite was at the other end. Eddie sat on one side of the table with the kids. Mr. P's attorney, Lloyd and Maxine Apple, and Karl Spink sat on the other side.

Right after the fabulous meal, the host addressed his guests about some details in his will. He began with Johnny. "Johnny, I'm leaving you my plane, Superland."

"Really?" the stunned pilot asked.

"You can't fly it until you get your license," the old pilot chuckled.

Johnny sat in stunned silence with his mouth agape. His mother beamed at him from across the table.

"Katie Spink," the smiling benefactor said as he turned to the freckle-faced gypsy, "your college education will be paid for by my estate."

Karl was humbled nearly to tears by the news, since Marilyn had taken half his net worth when she left him.

"Any college I want?" the gypsy asked her host.

"Yes!" Mr. P. answered emphatically. His attorney nodded in agreement.

Eddie could see that the rock star seated beside him was nervous about what was coming next.

"And Mickey ... everything else is yours."

Mickey was too shocked to speak.

Lloyd's mind was busy. He knew this news would devastate Marilyn, but it would give him more time to find Pond's last book that she was so desperate to get her hands on.

After dessert, they moved their chairs to the living room and sat before the roaring fire that Lloyd tended. Mickey stood facing the front window looking out at the flickering glow of pumpkins on the cliff line. His mind was racing with the incredible news that all of this would be his after his father died — a man he barely knew. He turned to the room and watched his father as he told old stories to his guests. *How can this be?* Mickey wondered. *Just a few months ago I was on that farm ... and had nothing.* He also knew that this news would devastate his mother, the same kind of selfish mother his father had.

Mickey slipped out of the house to get his amp and guitar from the barn. His generous father had requested that he play for his guests after dinner. Eddie went with Mickey out to the barn where the temperatures had dropped below freezing.

"I can't believe what he said to me," Mickey confessed to Eddie.

"Yes. You're one lucky dude," Eddie said.

"I know. I'm overwhelmed by it all."

"You should be. It's an overwhelming gift," Eddie smiled.
"Yeah."

Mickey played LAT 44 low, and it had a sweet melancholy sound throughout. Abbreviated to twenty-two minutes, the song was well-received by all. Even stiff Lloyd Apple got lost in his reverie during the song — knowing that once the old man was gone, Marilyn couldn't blackmail him any longer. He also realized that with Eddie and Mickey living at Prairieville, it would be impossible to find that book. LAT 44 made Lloyd see clearly that he had to break off his spying for the old man's ex-floorwalker.

When Mickey was done playing, Eddie overheard Lloyd's comment to his wife while the guests were applauding. "His mother's not going to be cheering ... that's for sure."

After reading *Superland,* Eddie knew more about Pond's handyman than most of the others in the room. And he knew that Mickey's mother would cause trouble for her son sooner or later once she got the news that her son was getting everything when the old man kicked the bucket. For Eddie, it was one more good reason to stay.

By the third week in November, when Wallis wanted to live more than ever, he came down with a bad cold that lingered. Wallis's nurse told her stubborn patient that she was taking him to a Dakota Falls hospital because his temperature indicated borderline pneumonia.

Eddie convinced Wallis to go to the hospital. "Remember, Wallis, you have too much to live for. Christmas, a new year, Mickey's graduation, and seeing Johnny get his pilot's license."

"I'll settle for Christmas," the old man chuckled and wheezed from his bed.

Of course, everyone who cared for Wallis was concerned about his health. When Marilyn heard from Lloyd about her ex-boss being hospitalized, she feared not bing able to talk to him about his estate and why he left her out of his will. She told Lloyd that it would be a good time to find that book. "And," she added, "his list of loyal readers. I know that's his most precious possession. He keeps it in a safe deposit box in his bank. Find that key to his box, Lloyd. Nobody can sell that book if I have that damn list. I'd still like to read that book, but I'd rather have the list. It's worth a few hundred to me if you can get me that key."

Poor Lloyd. He didn't want to do this for Marilyn, even though he could get some extra money for his trouble. He knew that she'd drag him to some motel before she paid him. And he'd better consider it paid in full — or else. "Or else" meant that she'd tell Wallis or Maxine about their flings. *That woman's got me by the kiwis and she won't let go,* he sniped to himself after unsuccessfully rifling through Pond's desk looking for a copy of *Superland* and the key to his safe deposit box.

Eddie had driven Mr. P to the hospital with Mickey riding along. Lloyd didn't want to open his boss's closed bedroom door, but he did.

No key or copy of the book was found in his bedroom. Inside the bedside table drawer, Lloyd found a wad of hundred-dollar bills but didn't take any of them. He knew that Wallis counted money and remembered every dollar. More than once Wallis caught his caretaker buying beer by the thirty-pack and charging it on his gas credit card. Lloyd knew that all the gas receipts were mailed to his estate attorney. However, Mr. P would see the receipt first and catch him every single time. "No way," Lloyd grumbled as he closed the bedside table drawer and left the room just the way he'd found it.

Every afternoon after school that week, Eddie and Mickey visited Wallis in his private room. The old man started improving right away, responding to medication so well that he would be released on Saturday. Marilyn debated whether to visit him at all, but she decided to by calling her son and telling him she would be driving Wallis home from the hospital on Saturday. Then she just hung up on the boy.

Marilyn showed up first thing Saturday morning in Wallis's room at the hospital. He wasn't surprised to hear her announce that she was taking him home. "I'm cutting your hair right now, too. It looks awful," she scoffed while running her manicured hand through his silver hair.

She helped him into his chair and removed her scissors, clippers and styling comb from her purse. Her small-talk to her gowned customer was what he expected. "So ... you're leaving everything to my son?" she asked with such spite and enmity in her voice that Wallis was frightened for a moment.

"I've given you hundreds of thousands of dollars ... not to mention twelve grand a year for eighteen years. Do you know how much money that is? It's over two hundred thousand dollars, Marilyn. You've gotten my money while I"m alive. My son will get my money when I'm gone."

"I suppose you don't remember last Christmas ... when you said I'd be taken care of when you're gone."

"That was before Mickey came into my life. Things have changed. I made a new will, and that has nothing to do with last Christmas."

The Cadman's white Cadillac parked in front of the house at Prairieville. Eddie helped Mr. P get into his chair after Mickey removed it from the trunk. Mickey and his mother didn't say a word to each other. She drove away as soon as Wallis was in his chair, and that was just fine with Mickey.

Wallis was elated to be home. Eddie had a fire going and had bought an expensive air purifier for Mr. P. "It's the best air purifier, and we can move it around the house," Eddie stated.

Wallis appreciated the gift since his nurse wanted him to get an oxygen tank mounted on his chair. "I'm not livin' here with tubes up my nose!" he'd barked at her, and the subject of oxygen was dropped.

Wallis slept well in his bed his first night home, feeling well enough the next day to watch Lucky and Johnny fly from his cliff line. The hawk sailed over Prairieville on air currents that Wallis guessed rose her to the cloud ceiling of at least a thousand feet. Johnny told the old aviator that the next Saturday would be his first flight with his instructor. If he passed, he was only eight weeks away from having his license and flying solo.

While Eddie prepared their lunch, Mickey was in his room reading the Wallis Pond novel that Katie had recently finished and was anxious for her brother to read. He was reading a chapter Katie had told him about, "Six-Dollar Dog."

I was fifteen and camped under a short railroad bridge that spanned a creek in the Oklahoma panhandle. The weather was freezing at night in November, and I had a grand fire going with nothing to eat. Two drifters came down from the tracks to get warm and hoped I had some food. They were lean and hungry with blazing blue eyes and dark weather-beaten faces, like most men living on the rails.

On and on they complained about the train that was overdue — the train that would take them to the golden hills of California where the food was plentiful and they could sleep under the warm sun all day if they wanted to.

I began to fear these men when they persisted in going back and forth between them that I was holding out food from them. They made me raise up my pant legs and open my coat where I might have concealed bread or precious meat.

From nowhere a scraggly, black mutt shepherd appeared near the edge of my fire. He too was lean and hungry and hoping for some food from three strangers. One of the men said, "Dog was good eatin' in lean times. I ate dog meat more than once."

"He's prob'ly some hobo's dog, and his master is likely to be close by," I volunteered, trying to sound brave.

"Naw! I seen many a dog attach to a man ... and the man dies ... and the dog drifts around lookin' for another man to take 'im in."

It all happened so fast, yet seemingly in slow motion. The men lured the dog over to them by calling for it while pretending to have food in their hands. I stood by, watching them hold the dog down until one of them got his boot on the side of the dog's neck and killed it without the slightest hesitation or guilt.

I left them my fire, not wanting any part of eating that dog. I wasn't as hungry as those men, and I questioned whether I could reach their level.

Between the tracks I walked west. Behind me I could hear the distant jubilation of hungry men preparing to eat. Right then I decided I'd never take a dog for a companion as many men do on the road. But I was kidding myself from the real thing that bothered me about seeing that dog killed so brutally. I could've stopped it by telling the men I'd give them all the money I had on me — six dollars. It was all I had to my name, and I feared starving if I let those men have it.

It kept bothering me that those men would've left that dog alone and high-tailed it to the next town to eat

*and drink like kings on my money. But I was not
attached to the dog, had no memories of it, and did not
care enough about its life to part with my six dollars.*

*Mile after mile I walked, the memory of that dog
haunting my every step in the darkness. I was not like
those men — oblivious to knowing that dog had been
someone's companion out here on these very tracks. He
had been a friend and a comfort to someone like me.
Someone who would think for him and feed him. Yes,
my own survival was threatened, and I caved in to my
own personal security as many might've done. Yet I still
had my six dollars, and it got me fed down the line.*

*Over the years on the road after that experience in
the Oklahoma panhandle, I gave dozens of dogs my
bread and meat in an attempt to make up for that
hungry night. That is a memory that has never left me
— and never will.*

Christmas morning at Prairieville Mickey awoke to find his
father in his chair at his desk. From his front window he showed
his son the new black Dodge Durango parked in front of his
house. He'd had the Marshall car dealer personally deliver it
earlier in the morning. Wallis handed Mickey the keys to his
new vehicle and told him he wanted to go along on his test drive.

Eddie rode along in the backseat of the new vehicle, seeing
up close the pleasure on the faces of both father and son.

"I can't believe this is mine," Mickey kept saying. The
laughter from Wallis said that he was getting so much more in
return for the generous gift to his son. Mickey knew as well as
Eddie that Wallis wanted his son to enjoy his money while he
was alive to see it.

Wallis's words to Eddie the night before were clear as they
sat on the sofa enjoying a glass of wine in front of the fire. "The
fact that he's my son ... that's everything." He told Eddie he was
having the Durango delivered to Prairieville Christmas morning.

Mickey drove country roads, highways, and the main drags
of Kenwick, LeRoy and Marshall on his test drive. Wallis was
pleased with Mickey's driving. The boy confessed to his father

that he'd been driving since he was eleven, often taking Ned's car on quick rides on the road in front of the farm while his aged guardian slept in front of the television set.

Eddie and Mickey saw Wallis remove a gas credit card from his wallet and hand it to the stunned driver. "You're insured with my insurance carrier in Dakota Falls ... so be careful."

"Oh, I will. I will, Dad."

That one word — dad — made everything worthwhile to Wallis. He had never said that word to his own father.

The generosity displayed and respect returned were obvious to Eddie. It made him recall Wallis Pond's last chapter in *Superland* titled "Different."

I want my son to be different from me and start out his young adulthood with money. That is the best gift I can give him. His mother will not get a dime from me when I'm gone. I just cannot reward the same kind of woman my mother was when I leave this world.

I hope he spends his money wisely — much better than I did. The best money I ever spent was for his monthly care on a farm for eighteen years. I actually felt good every time I wrote his support check. I knew that at least in some remote way he had heard from me.

If I am fortunate enough to meet my son before I die, I will show him that I can be generous. I want to convey that I always meant well and thought about his well-being. I know what it's like to be young and broke all the time. I've often said that the lack of money is the root of all evil.

Not knowing how many years, if any, I have left has made me realize that I can start again through my son. He will not lack the money I did and have such a tough go of it.

Throughout his life I was unable to give him my name — for my own selfish reasons. I would be proud of him with or without my name because he has taken what he's been given in this world and will go his way. But he won't be alone. My money will be there to show him I felt concern for my son's welfare. That's how I am different from my father.

Night Flight

By the end of January, Johnny would acquire his pilot's license. His final flight with his instructor was a night flight whereupon he could only rely on his instrument readings. The flight went well, flying over the lights of Kenwick and Prairieville. Thirty minutes later, after a perfect landing at Marshall Airfield, Johnny Apple was a licensed pilot. After taxying into the hanger and shaking hands with Wade Hampton, Johnny felt like he had accomplished something big.

During the flight, Wade had offered to buy Superland from his student for thirty thousand dollars. Johnny said he wasn't interested in selling, at least for the time being. He reminded his instructor he wouldn't even inherit the vintage plane until its present owner had died.

But flying is expensive. Johnny knew he's need money for fuel and at least a hundred bucks an hour for every time he flew. He had to keep adding to his hours of flight time, flying different kinds of single- and twin-engine aircraft. That's where the big money was — flying CEOs around the country in corporate jets. And building up flight time took money.

Mr. P was the first person Johnny showed his diploma and license certification. The old man shook his hand and told the young pilot he had accomplished something that very few men attained.

It was Lloyd who told his understanding boss about Johnny's situation. Right away Wallis made arrangements for the new pilot to get in three hours of flight time a month at his expense. "That'll keep him sharp until he graduates from high school," Pond told his grateful caretaker.

Later that evening, Wallis expressed his true feelings to Eddie. "I don't want Lloyd to think I"m doing this for him. I'm doing it for the boy. Some company from Minneapolis or

Dakota Falls could take him on and train him to fly their planes ... if he puts his feelers out there. I'm glad Mickey has no interest in flying. It's a dangerous way to make a living. It's safer than driving, but every year hundreds of planes go down and people get killed. I was one of the lucky ones."

Johnny was restless through February and March, no longer interested in flying his radio-controlled planes from the cliff line. Mickey had legally changed his last name to Pond with the help of his father's attorney. Mickey Pond wanted to drive Johnny the one-hundred miles to Yankton, South Dakota, where Johnny was going to release Lucky into the wild at Yankton Dam. Johnny had heard that hawks flourished there and were protected from hunters.

Lucky rode in the back of the new Durango inside her cage on the Sunday morning they made the journey. It was during the drive to Yankton that Johnny told Mickey how he found Lucky.

Johnny had been flying from the cliff line in early May while his dad was removing storm windows from the house at Prairieville. It had been a rough winter with twice the average snowfall and lingering winter temperatures until early May. Lloyd and Johnny both heard the distinct sound of a rifle shot north of the barn. Then they heard a second. Trespassing boys with guns were often run off from Prairieville by the caretaker. They were cowards who would shoot anything living — birds, rabbits, deer, even stray cats and dogs.

Lloyd, a two-year veteran of the Marine Corps, had no patience for "those little cowards with guns." He had often told his son, "They're fearful and mean little boys with s— for brains."

When Johnny saw his dad stalking off in the direction of the rifle shots, he kept his plane flying while walking fast down the slope of the cliff line. Off to the north some three hundred yards, Lloyd could see that two boys had fired their rifles into the high branches of a blue spruce that bordered Kenwick Road. They had fired up into the tree, aiming at a thirty-six-inch-diameter nest made by a red-tailed hawk.

The boys ignored Lloyd's distant warning: "HEY! GET OUTTA THERE!" They continued firing into the nest.

Johnny had the idea to fly his plane over to the boys to distract them by buzzing them with dive bombs. However, the pilot at the controls had to keep moving because he only had radio frequency control up to two hundred yards with this model. So he caught up with his father, passed him, and full-throttled his engine until the boys and their weapons vanished into the tree line and off Mr. P's property.

He landed his plane on high prairie grass without sustaining much damage. The Apples went over to the tree where the boys had fired into the nest. There on the ground lay the dead mother, a beautiful red-tailed hawk with its breast bloody from a .22. Lloyd used his boot to turn the bird over. Her underparts were a pale brown with dark brown streaks, and she had a light auburn tail that was fanned out and fluttering in the breeze. With his boot Lloyd exposed the curved black beak and razor-sharp talons of the twenty-four-inch-long bird of prey.

"See there? They can shred a rabbit to pieces. It's a chicken hawk ... related to buzzards. It's one tough raptor," he told his son.

He followed his father's eyes up to a nest that was thirty feet above them and wedged in the fork of a large branch. He could see his father tracing a climb with his eyes and rightfully discerning that he could never make the climb. He told his son, "If you make that climb and find a live chick ... you'll have to raise it ... or it'll die."

Without hesitation, Johnny climbed the tree with the dexterity of an ape. Before going out onto the branch, he tested it by standing and then bouncing his weight on it. Then he eased his way out until he had to straddle it and slide himself forward by pulling his arms and moving further and further out onto the solid branch.

When he was finally able to see inside the nest, there was a lone chick with a fuzzy dark-brown coat of downy feathers and a bald head that was not even close to resembling the plumage its mother had. It was alive and still blind, unable to stand or move about the nest. The nest itself was the size of a large sombrero his mother gave him when he was five.

"One chick! Alive!"

His father was blunt. "Kill it or keep it!" He explained later that other birds would kill it, or it would starve to death.

Johnny knew that he could never wring the chick's neck, so he reached for the orphan and raked it gently into his palm. He slipped it inside his shirt pocket and delivered it to the ground much sooner than its mother had planned. On the ground he exclaimed, "It's alive, Dad!"

"That's one lucky bird," Lloyd groaned when kneeling to pluck feathers from its dead mother. "You'll have to build a cage and a nest. Mama's feathers will be its bed."

"Lucky," Johnny repeated. Then he announced he would name the bird Lucky. "Can you tell if it's a boy or a girl?" he asked his father.

"Can't tell. Both sexes look alike. I know adult females are bigger than the males."

On their walk back to the barn, Johnny was excited because his dad said there were plenty of materials in the barn, including mesh screen left over from replacing some of Mr. P's window screens. Lloyd said his son could make a fine cage for the bird and that his mother's garden in the Apple backyard would supply plenty of worms "for the little buzzard."

Still inside Johnny's shirt pocket, Lucky chirped as if the mention of worms had aroused its appetite.

Lloyd grinned to himself because he was proud of his boy for buzzing "those idiots" and for making something good happen from such a senseless act.

Mickey and Johnny stood on top of the Yankton Dam. Spring's muddy slush churned the river water to a green-brown frenzy as Lucky perched on her handler's gloved hand waiting to be released. Mickey said, "Goodbye, Lucky," and touched her beak.

Then Johnny said, "Have a good life, Lucky. You're free now."

He kissed the air and raised his hand for her to fly away. They watched her for only a few moments before returning to the Durango and driving away.

Outside of Yankton on their way to Vermillion, Mickey asked his quiet friend if he was okay.

"Yeah ... I'm okay."

Gas was over three bucks a gallon in late April, so prudent Mickey Pond rode his bike to school — which really impressed his father. Pedaling past the Spink house on his way to school, he saw Katie and Karl leaving the house on their way to school and work.

Katie told her brother that their mother called last night to tell her she was going into a cancer treatment center in Dakota Falls to have tumors removed from her colon.

"Her cancer is back?" Mickey asked.

"Yeah ... but they won't know how much it's spread until they open her up," Karl said.

None of the trio felt real sorry for Marilyn or felt any desire to visit her in the hospital. Katie said, "When she told me, I didn't feel anything at all. I just wished her well. Then she told me, 'If anything happens to me, I want you to have all my furniture and things in storage.' I don't want any of her things," Katie said to her father and Mickey.

Mickey felt the same as Katie. "When I lived on the farm, Bert had a friend who had cancer. Bert said that cancer was caused by anger and resentment ... and that 'anger' is one letter from 'danger.'"

"Yeah, I can believe that. She's always been mad at somebody," Karl said as they turned onto Main.

"It's like Mr. P's mother. Selfish people," Katie commented.

"I don't even know if I ever really believed she had cancer. She'd lie all the time about being sick when she was s'posed to pick me up at the farm."

"I just don't feel sorry for her at all ... and she's my mother," Katie said.

"Yeah ... me too," Mickey agreed.

Karl wanted to change the subject because he was still reeling from Marilyn telling him in her cold manner that their divorce was final now. She had received her copy of the filed papers from her attorney. Karl was not bold enough to ask Marilyn if she planned on leaving Katie her half of his retirement savings she'd withdrawn from the bank when she left him.

It was an especially long Monday at school for Mickey and Katie. They kept thinking about their mother possibly dying of cancer and all the unspoken words between them. Since Mickey and Katie were reading titles ten and eleven in the Billy Lake series, they were aware of the difficulty Wallis had his whole life because of his unresolved relationship with his mother.

After school that day, Mickey rode his bike slowly beside his pedestrian sister on their way home. Mickey said, "If it's real ... if she really has cancer ... I think we should go visit her at the hospital."

Yeah ... maybe we should. I'd like Eddie to go with us."

"Yeah, he'd be good with the whole scene."

"I could get some flowers at the florist in LeRoy," Katie suggested.

"Yeah, that might be good. I guess I could drive us there. Do you think your dad would want to go with us?" Mickey asked.

"No. Remember what Mr. P wrote about how Billy's father would have nothing more to do with Edna?" Well, that's how my father feels about my mom. He wants nothing to do with her."

Mickey drove Katie and Eddie to the city to visit Marilyn after picking up a bouquet of yellow and white daisies at the florist. Katie said her mother loved daisies because they always cheered her up.

Eddie decided to get a bite to eat in the hospital cafeteria, giving the kids private time with their mother.

They entered her private room like children facing their punishment with grim uncertainty. Katie put the vase of daisies on her mother's bedside table.

The patient said, "They're lovely." She told her children she was having additional surgery the next morning. A foot of her intestines was to be removed. Her doctor believed that was as far as the cancer had spread.

Mickey had never seen his mother without makeup or her hair perfect. She looked old and tired to him. Then Mickey shocked his mother and Katie by asking Marilyn who she was most angry with. "It could be part of your cancer ... I've heard," he added.

Marilyn surprised them with her resigned answer, as if at peace with herself, "Oh, I've been angry most of my life. My parents ... as you know," she patted Mickey's hand, "were not so easy to live with."

Mickey nodded, knowing exactly what she meant.

Katie's eyes teared when her mother told her that the money she had in the bank would go to her. "Mickey, you've been taken care of by Wallis ... that's for sure."

"Could that be part of your anger?" he asked her.

"Oh ... it's probably kept things moving. When I first met Wallis, he always treated me special. I'd never been treated like that by a man before. I guess I always thought he'd remember me in other ways besides writing about me in some book. Have you read his last book?" she asked them.

They shook their heads, indicating they hadn't.

"Well, I don't care anymore if he publishes it ... and I want you to tell Lloyd Apple that for me ... please. Will you do that?"

They both nodded yes.

"And tell Wallis I have no bad feelings toward him."

More nodding.

Then she did what Wallis always wanted her to do. "I want both of you to know I'm sorry for not being the mother you needed ... and for leaving both of you."

Katie cried. Mickey held his mother's hand. Forgiveness was all over that private hospital room.

Before they left her room, Marilyn said to Katie, "Please tell Karl how sorry I am. I hope he can forgive me for all the awful things I did to him when we were married."

They each gave her a goodbye kiss on the cheek, and she told them she loved them. They left her room and met Eddie in the waiting area.

Eddie consoled Katie, for the contrite words her mother had told them had touched her. Mickey related to Eddie everything their mother had said to them, and both he and Katie decided they would come back again Tuesday after school.

Tuesday afternoon as he was just returning from his lunch break, Karl received a call at the elevator from the Cadman. The car dealer told Karl that Marilyn had died during surgery. Her cancer was too far advanced and her body gave out.

Karl walked home early from work and called Wallis to give him the news about his ex-floorwalker. Wallis was stunned and asked Eddie to drive him to the school after picking up Karl. He wanted them all to be there when school let out. Eddie and Karl stood by the front door of the school when the bell rang. Mr. P waited in Eddie's car.

Mickey exited the school with Johnny. Karl told Mickey that his mother had passed away during surgery, and Eddie helped Mickey load his bike into the trunk of the car.

Katie came outside and her father broke the news to her. He consoled his daughter and sat with her and Mickey in the backseat of Eddie's car after Johnny said he would walk home.

Wallis didn't say a word until after they'd parked in the Spink driveway. The kids stood close to the open front passenger door so the old man could talk to them. He told them that their mother always wanted her ashes left in Prairieville, and that they could do that from the cliff line for her service. Wallis focused on Katie as Mickey stood with her in the warm afternoon sun.

"Your mother got to tell you things yesterday that I always wanted her to tell you ... especially after she left you and Karl. You can grow strong from this if you focus on those positive things said yesterday. But I'll tell you this ... if you dwell on negative things in your past, you will diminish yourself and never have a chance to live your life in the light."

Katie went into her house with her father after the others drove away. She sat on Karl's lap in his recliner, and they both had a good cry.

Mickey told his father he was okay and that he'd already decided to live his life in the light. Right away he went into the cool barn, turned on his amp, and played LAT 44 in a new way that Eddie and Wallis had not heard him play before.

Eddie and Wallis remained outside near the front door of the house for twenty minutes listening to the song that Mickey had now spent hundreds if not thousands of hours playing. LAT 44 was bringing back to Wallis his fondest memory of Marilyn. It was the day he'd first met her, the day she picked out his walking cane. He wished he had written more about that lunch date with Marilyn in *Superland* upon hearing from the kids what she'd said about his book and the fact that she obviously had wanted Lloyd to get the book for her to read. After the kids told Wallis about what she had asked them to tell his caretaker, Wallis told the kids he wanted to relay Marilyn's words to Lloyd himself.

Wallis called Lloyd on his cell phone, wanting his caretaker to get the catering handled for twenty people attending Marilyn's service at Prairieville on Saturday. "And after the service, I want to talk to you about Marilyn."

The call from his boss caused Lloyd to drink more, doing shots of Johnny Walker Red with his beer. For two nights in a row, he passed out on the front seat of the truck and spent the night there.

Maxine was livid. Arguing at the supper table about his drinking binges was only a smokescreen for the upcoming "talk about Marilyn" Mr. P wanted to have Saturday. Johnny was so tired of hearing their verbal battles that during each meal he left the table with his plate and ate in his room.

Friday night Mickey invited Johnny and Katie over to hear his new version of LAT 44 that he was going to play at his mother's service the next day. Johnny told Katie he'd pick her up at seven-thirty, and they'd walk over to the barn and be there by eight.

For three nights in a row, Lloyd was awol after supper and staggered home hung over just before his son got up for school. At supper Friday night, Lloyd swore to his wife that he wasn't going to drink, that he wanted to be clean and sober for the service the next day.

At seven-thirty, it was just light enough to cut through Prairieville, entering close to the pond. Johnny griped to Katie about how the arguing at home between his parents because of his father drinking was driving him crazy. "He's got some big-time problem going on ... and alcohol is how he drowns it. But it never really drowns. It keeps coming back with more and more pain."

"Eddie said that any addiction begins and ends in pain," Katie said.

"Yeah ... no kidding."

Johnny told Katie that at the supper table he asked his dad about whether he should ask Mr. P if he could fly over Prairieville in a rented Piper Cub from the Marshall Airfield. "It would only cost a hundred bucks plus fuel, and I could scatter her ashes from five hundred feet all over Prairieville."

What'd he say?" Katie asked.

"He hit the roof! He started yellin' about Mr. P not lettin' him keep workin' at Prairieville after Mr. P dies. And how ungrateful the old bastard is. 'No way! If he don't want me, he ain't gettin' my son to fly over Prairieville either! So don't bother me about doin' such a stupid thing,' he said."

"Wow ... that's harsh," Katie empathized. "It could've been something special for my mom if you did that."

"Yeah ... but don't mention it to anybody, okay?

"Okay."

When they reached the barn the door was open. Mr. P and Eddie were there watching Mickey set up for his rehearsal. Eddie had brought out three folding chairs, two of which were for Katie and Johnny and positioned facing Mickey inside the doorway.

This was a special moment for Mickey. He had memorized spacings in LAT 44 for his mother's service. That's what Eddie had told Mickey he liked about his song. "It's the space between the notes that the listener gets lost in. That space is when the listener emotes, feels the song ... and has a chance to show how the busy mind can be stopped ... if you pay attention to the gaps between notes."

"Sweet," Mickey had replied to Eddie's comment.

All were seated and he began playing LAT 44, his "self" paying more attention than ever to the gaps. The gaps were Mickey Pond's past — when he was Mickey Ditwell, the cynical loner. He would live for those gaps his mother gave him, brief respites from the farm and Ned and Bert's dead faces. Now the gaps were there, between the notes of his life. Some were short gaps, like when his mother didn't show to take him Christmas shopping or a dozen other times. Then there were longer gaps, when he'd spend the whole day with her and return home to the farm to continue playing the same tune she had written for him.

About seven minutes into LAT 44, the jagged shadow of Lloyd Apple cast itself in the deepest ravine on Prairieville, some seventy yards from the back of the barn. After drinking a pint of Johnny Walker Red after supper, he tried to stagger home and fell down into the ravine. He had been sober all day. Face-up at the bottom of the ravine, he stared up at the crescent moon above him. He listened to the haunting music riding the winds across Prairieville. All the negative things were there — the motel room with Marilyn, the money she paid him, and worst of all that damn book she wanted. He too would be in that book for Maxine and his son to read. They would hate him. And that old bastard would leave him without work — or without mention in his will.

The gaps in the song got to Lloyd Apple. He could see clearly how he betrayed his family and the generous man who had hired him on when he lost his job as the county garbage collector. He thought of how his old customer Wallis Pond had offered him a job as caretaker, even though he had to know he'd been fired for drinking on his route.

"Yep," he mumbled and began to sob with the music, sinking lower and lower into the depths of his pain. Then he thought about Saturday, after the service, when he had to confess it all to Mr. P and beg him not to print what he and Marilyn did.

He tried to stand from his knees, but LAT 44 pressed on him. It's haunting notes drove him up and out of the ravine. Back to the bar.

Later, after closing time, he was the last person in the bar. He left the front and back doors unlocked. He was prepared for this moment.

Early Saturday morning, Johnny told his mother he'd go to the bar to see if his father had spent another night in the truck parked behind the bar. The truck was there, but empty. He entered the bar via the back door but didn't see any sign of anybody. The basement door was open. After checking the men's room he called down into the basement, "DAD?"

He followed the steps down to the lit basement and found his father right away — hanging dead from a rope attached to a sewer pipe. A chair was kicked over and away from where the body hung. Johnny ran to his father but could not untie the knot behind his dad's neck. He stood on the chair, trembling as he tried to lift the limp body up with one arm and undo the knot with the other. He ran upstairs, grabbed a butcher's knife, and cut his father gently down to the cold cement floor.

He thought of his mother and started to cry. Then he went upstairs to call the sheriff's office.

Fallen Apples

Of course Maxine was in shock. She loved her husband and never dreamed he'd do such a thing.

The news of Lloyd Apple's suicide was all over Kenwick and LeRoy. Marilyn's service went on as scheduled, minus three guests. Mickey played his song as the host and Eddie watched from the front wheelchair ramp. Katie and Karl scattered Marilyn's remains from atop the cliff line.

Earlier that morning when the Cadman delivered Marilyn's urn of ashes, Wallis told him he wasn't welcome to attend the service since Katie and her father would be there. The car dealer left after giving Wallis the key to Marilyn's storage locker and the access code to the storage lot. When Pond asked him about Marilyn's cash in her savings account, the Cadman graciously said that all her assets would be turned over to Katie by Marilyn's attorney in Dakota Falls. And as far as Marilyn's clothes and jewelry and things in the house, he would make sure Katie got everything she wanted from her mother's estate.

Everyone's thoughts at the service were on Johnny and Maxine. "Such a cowardly way out," Wallis had scoffed to Eddie and Mickey when the Spinks came by to deliver the grim news about Lloyd Apple. "And to have his son find him hanging in the basement of the Kenwick Tavern. Ah ... it's awful," Wallis grumbled.

Eddie could see right away that Johnny would need professional counseling — and the sooner the better. He mentioned to Pond about all three kids getting therapy to handle their grief.

The old man didn't hesitate. "Find a good therapist in Dakota Falls and I'll pay for it. And Maxine too ... if she'll go."

Again Eddie was amazed at Wallis Pond's generosity. The old man thought about how he'd told Lloyd in foreboding words that he wanted to talk to him about Marilyn, so he knew he played a part in Lloyd's decision to take his life. This made him think again about his last book that was stored in his secret place in Superland, a gift to Lloyd's son.

The things he wrote about in *Superland* that would hurt Johnny and Maxine were in a chapter near the end of the book called "Things Billy Knew."

When Marilyn left Karl, Lloyd, my alcoholic handyman, was sleeping with Marilyn. Or rather, doing everything but sleeping with her. I started getting my tips from Harold, owner of the Kenwick Motel where Lloyd and Marilyn got together for their "business meetings." Harold's wife is a graduate of my beauty college, and I appreciate his quick calls to me at least six or seven times a month.

And I know for certain that Marilyn wouldn't want this chapter in my last book. Betrayal, spying, lying to people who care for your welfare — all of these are things Billy Lake could never tolerate. Yet I wish neither of them malice or retribution, for I am fond of Lloyd's son, Johnny, who will fly Superland one day. And, of course, Marilyn is the mother of my only child. She is also the mother of Katie, a bright-eyed bundle of potential I'm also very fond of.

I hope the sex was worth it, Lloyd. Maybe someday you'll sober up and see what a jerk you were.

As for Marilyn, I hope you resolve your relationship with your children.

* * * * *

Johnny called Wallis Pond from his kitchen phone while his mother grieved amidst a huge backlog of ironing brought in by well-meaning locals. Many brought sympathy cards with their clothing.

"Mr. P? Johnny Apple."

"Johnny ... how are you?"

"Oh, I'm fine. Kinda numb, I guess."

"How's your mother doing?"

"Oh ... the same ... I guess."

"What can I do for ya, Johnny?"

"Mr. P, I wanted to ask you if I could fly over Prairieville and scatter my dad's ashes. I'd rent a Piper Cub ... single engine ... and it would only cost me a hundred and fifty bucks with fuel."

"That's fine, Johnny. I think that's a good idea. I'll call Jake at the airfield tomorrow and tell him to set you up and send me the bill."

"Thanks, Mr. P ... but I wasn't callin' to see if you'd pay for it. My mom would pay for it."

I know, son. I want to do it."

"Thank you."

"You're welcome. So your mother's okay with the idea?"

"Oh, yeah. She doesn't want his ashes around the house, and it'll save money by not having to bury him."

"Uh-huh. When are you planning to fly over?"

"I don't know. He's already been cremated. Soon though."

"I'll call Jake, then I'll let ya know when it's been set up."

"Thanks, Mr. P."

"Oh ... and Johnny?"

"Yeah?"

"I want ya to do something for me."

"Sure ... you name it."

"I can pay for a top-notch therapist in the City for you and your mother. Katie and Mickey already told me they'd go."

"Yeah? I'd go. But I don't know about my mom."

"Well ... wait awhile ... and when the time's right you can ask her."

"Okay. I will."

"Good. Will be in touch. Bye, Johnny."

"Bye, Mr. P. Thanks for everything."

"Keep flying, boy."

"I will."

Two days later it was all arranged for Johnny to fly a Piper Cub for an hour so he could drop his father's ashes over Prairieville. Wade told Wallis Pond on the phone that Jake, the owner of the airfield, paid for it and would see that their recent graduate got the best.

Johnny flew over Prairieville and released his father's remains from a container Wade gave him. The flight was on a school day in the late morning. His focus was on the flight and the symbolic gesture that Prairieville was a special place for his father.

Maxine watched her son fly over her house at an altitude of about five hundred feet in the little plane that was white with blue trim. She waved and watched her son fly over Prairieville. He told her later that evening that he had emptied the ashes out of his cockpit window when he was directly over the cliff line.

Pond and Eddie watched him fly over, then circle around and fly over the cliff line again on his return flight to the airfield. Johnny had called Mr. P with his flight plan, and the old aviator was more than thrilled to see the boy who once flew radio-controlled gliders from his cliff line now flying as a licensed pilot.

The Kenwick Public School lunchroom was packed on graduation day when Johnny and Mickey received their diplomas from the principal. Tearful Maxine sat with the Spinks, Wallis and Eddie. The applause was loud when Johnny's name was called to receive his diploma, and the same was true a bit later when Mickey received his.

"What're you gonna do now?" Johnny asked Mickey.

"Play my music ... travel."

"Where you goin'?"

"I don't know. I might have to get a job."

"You're rich, man. You don't have to work."

"I s'pose ... What're you gonna do?"

"I gotta get a job to pay for my flying."

"My dad's payin' for your flyin'."

"Yeah, but I want to fly more ... so I can get a good gig flying execs around the country. I'll have to go to school to learn how to fly jets."

"My dad would help ya."

"Yeah ... but ..."

"Yeah but yer stupid if ya don't ask him."

Katie came over to the graduates and hugged them, then all three returned to where Mr. P, Maxine, Eddie and Karl were standing. Maxine broke down again, hugging and kissing her son on this special day.

Mickey's only year in a public school had flown by. He now had the confidence to keep improving LAT 44 without a timetable or deadline. He told his father that he didn't want to go to college. He wasn't ready for that kind of environment away from the home at Prairieville he'd come to love.

This was graduation day for Wallis also. He had lived to see his son graduate with Johnny. Marilyn and Lloyd were gone, and Eddie was writing his second novel. Mickey, Eddie and Wallis had stayed up late the night before making plans for the future. Mickey expressed his desire to stay home for the summer to play his music and work on the projects his dad had in mind for him around Prairieville.

"You would earn your wages, of course ... and then you'd have traveling money ... unless you wanted to go to Europe," Pond chuckled.

The mention of Europe gave Mickey an idea. Wallis's father was Irish, and Mickey thought he'd like to visit Ireland to see his family's heritage. "How much would it cost to go to Ireland?" he asked his father.

"Oh, I s'pose a round-trip coach flight would cost about a grand. Summer's a peak time around there for tourists."

"Well, if I worked thirty hours a week at eight bucks an hour — like you said — that's two hundred and forty a week. If I can work for eight or ten weeks straight ... I'd have enough," Mickey smiled.

Wallis was elated with Mickey's idea to explore Ireland. Young Wallis had gone there a few years after opening his beauty college. He'd spent most of his time in Dublin scouring pubs, looking for his father to no avail. However, he did have fond memories of a few girls he met over there — girls he had stayed in touch with to the present day.

After Mickey went to bed, Wallis and Eddie continued their discussion about the future. Eddie wasn't as clear as Mickey was about his plans for the summer. "Maybe I can hold onto my book ... keep it moving."

"That's right," Pond slapped his thigh, "keep it moving forward. I like to focus on one chapter at a time ... not the entire book. And I like to be surprised ... and have the ending come to me late in the story." The prolific writer of twenty-seven novels did not want to know what Eddie's story was about. For Wallis, it always somehow diminished the story to talk about it, so he never did.

After the deaths of Marilyn and Lloyd, *Superland* was not important and was put on hold. Wallis said that if the kids wanted to read it after they got counseling, so be it. Besides, ever since Mickey came into Pond's life, it no longer seemed important to the author to publish his last book. Wallis had told Eddie one evening, "I wrote about Marilyn and Lloyd to get some kind of revenge ... even if it was from the grave. Now ... things have changed."

Wallis had made it up to Eddie by giving him the money he would have earned by selling *Superland* to his loyal readers. Now that the former cab driver had more money in the bank than he ever dreamed of, he told his generous benefactor, "Now that I can go anywhere and do anything, I don't know where I want to go or what I'd do when I got there."

The old man chuckled in his knowing way and said, "I know what you mean. Until Prairieville found me, I pretty much felt the same way. Have you considered publishing your second book now that you have the funds to do so?"

"Not the same way as before. I don't have a list of readers, and I'm not going to beat myself up like that again. I'm too old for that," Eddie smiled at his favorite author.

"What about selling your book to my readers, using my list and route? I could even write a review for your back cover."

That's when Eddie told Pond that he had the idea to have Mickey put LAT 44 on a CD that could be sold with his book. "But selling my book to your readers along with your son's music ... that just sounds too easy," Eddie smiled.

"If it ain't easy, Eddie ... don't do it," Pond chuckled.

After the graduation ceremonies were over and Eddie and Wallis were back at Prairieville, Eddie pondered the old man's offer from the night before. He was humbled by Wallis's generosity — not only to himself, but also for the three kids he adored. "Ya know, Mr. P ... you have been most generous to me and those kids. I think while I'm here workin' on my book, I could get you some weights and help you tone up those long arms and legs of yours."

The old man thought about it for a few seconds and said, "Ya know, that might be a good idea ... to put some muscle back on these old bones for the coming winter. My nurse has been wanting me to do that for years. I think I'll take you up on that offer. If I know someone else is puttin' in effort for me ... I'll stay with it. I don't think I'd ever do something like that alone. Yet alone is not all that bad, Eddie. In my books I made Billy the hard luck story — him against the world ... the abandoned loner who wanted to make something of himself without anyone's help. Now that I'm old, I'm not alone anymore. I've been lucky to see my son in my life and to have a new friend like you.

Eddie was humbled to teary eyes, telling his wise mentor, "I've learned so much from you in your books ... and so much in the short time I've been here. But there's one thing I want to do. When you were my age you were living the high life ... dating beautiful women, successful in business, flying all over the country. I don't have that kind of living in me and haven't had it since I broke up with my first love, Lauren, in California. Somewhere in my past I'm holding onto things you lived through and were able to move on and forgive. Forgiveness to me is letting things and words pass through you ... not holding onto them. I want to go see that therapist in the city and see what I can find out."

"Well, you might get some good results from therapy. I sure did. I found out I had used things and words as fuel to prove my parents wrong ... that I was worth keeping. Forgiveness came much later in my life ... after therapy ... when I had been to Galena to visit my mother."

"Oh, yeah. I liked that chapter. How you had to climb those awful hills and steps in Galena with your knees in such pain. I can see it so clearly even now," Eddie smiled.

"When I think of Galena, I think of Sam Grant and how he must've enjoyed a cold beer like I did that day. And I know if I'd had one more beer that day, I may not have ever gone to see her."

"Oh, yes you would've. It was something you had to do ... for you and Billy."

"Yeah, you're right, Mr. Dense," Pond laughed quietly. Then his face got serious and he said, "I still can't help but think that my visit with her hastened her death somehow. I just don't know whether it gave her any kind of peace as it did for me. And even with Lloyd Apple ... I know I prob'ly hastened his death too on some level."

"I don't think Johnny or Maxine would believe that for one second. I know I don't."

"If they read *Superland* they might believe it."

"I don't agree. Lloyd was in the pain body big time. I could see that. And it wasn't caused by some book he'd never read."

"Just the same, I've arranged for my accountant to send Maxine Lloyd's check every week. I'm good at writing a check to diminish my guilt," Pond said.

"That's generous, Mr. P."

"Johnny'll have a little money in his pocket from his old man's checks, I'm certain."

"That's great. Whaddaya say to ridin' over with me to a Marshall sporting goods store to get those weights?"

"Now?"

"If not now ... when?" Eddie grinned.

The old man laughed and motored his way outside to Eddie's car. Life was improving at Prairieville.

* * * * *

Pond put his son to work painting the barn a barnwood gray, Wallis's favorite color. Eddie helped here and there by positioning the twenty-five-foot extension ladder while Mickey was busy stripping off the old paint.

Wallis would go out to the barn twice a day to work out with the barbell set Eddie bought him. Eddie would do sets of repetitions with the old writer that focused on his biceps, triceps and wrists. Wallis was determined to do what his trainer wanted. Eddie would hold a light barbell over each of Wallis's feet, and he would do leg lifts. Shoulder presses were the hardest for the old man, when he'd raise a weight with each hand above his head. Then they worked neck and chest muscles. Eddie started him very light at first; he wanted to get the old man's muscles used to the new motions demanded of his body after so many years of atrophy from inactivity.

Meanwhile, Wade got Johnny a job detailing private planes at the airfield for thirty hours a week. And Johnny met a girl. Hanna just graduated from Marshall High, and she was also certified by Wade Hampton to fly single-engine planes. Johnny met Hanna in the airfield hangar when he was detailing her father's jet — one of the more expensive aircraft at the airfield. They talked often about flying, and Johnny asked her if she wanted to fly with him sometime.

"Only if I can drive," the attractive brunette smiled.

"Oh, no ... I need my hours."

She liked Johnny's straightforward manner. And he liked everything about Hanna.

Johnny was also obligated to haul Mr. P's garbage for him, since the old man told him he could use his truck to drive back and forth to work, as long as he carried his own insurance.

With wheels, a job, and a potential new girlfriend, Johnny was looking forward to his first counseling session in the city. Katie was going with him because her first session was just before his.

Mickey was happily at work painting the old barn that would one day be his. He and Eddie also had back-to-back sessions with the same therapist in a few days. Life was good at Prairieville in many ways.

Mr. P was cooking more — preparing meals in his kitchen and grilling on his back deck. His exercise regimen with the weights was giving him more energy and he felt like doing more. He'd roll out to the barn wearing his Panama hat and deliver lemonade and protein bars to his son. Mickey would gulp down the cold drink while his dad noticed the work he'd done, commenting exactly on the progress made since his last trip out. That really impressed his helper and motivated him even more.

Eddie would write in his room at a small desk that faced the front of the house. His book had no title yet. He was working on a chapter he titled "Summer at Prairieville." Taking a break from his book, he had written a letter to his mother and sister, often using some of the passages he'd written for the book.

My life at Prairieville is going so well that I can hardly believe I drove a cab for so long. I want you to know that I've never been happier than I am now. I could write three hundred pages describing Prairieville, this place where I live for now. But then another season would come and it would change, like an interstice — or, rather, the small spacing between things would also change. In June there is the white clover and yellow sweet clover that Mr. P would point out to me. Then again, he would point out a swath of purple vetch or bull thistle growing in spaces of red clover.

As you know, my favorite writer is in a wheelchair — a fancy motorized one that moves faster than I can walk. He has extensively researched all the flowers and birds that live here, finding them with his binoculars and matching them up with colorful photos of birds in a rather large aviary book.

It's not surprising to me that Mr. P is interested in birds, since he flew his own plane for many years when he was a young man.

Recently, the "old man" had me look through his binoculars at a bird feeder not far from his front window. Rusty blackbirds would chase away the American goldfinch from the seed Mr. P would put out every morning. He would get up early with the birds and see a different aviary show every single morning that could fill a hundred pages. When the mean black crows would chase off the blue jays, Mr. P would patiently wait. After some twenty minutes, those blue jays would return in such greater numbers that the crows would eventually give up their seed. "Jays are smart and violent," the old man would quip. "If I was a bird ... I'd stay clear of those jays."

Mickey Pond is another "boarder" here. Now, there's an interesting cat if I've ever seen one. He came here shortly after his eighteenth birthday to meet his father (Mr. P) for the first time in his life. I cannot help but marvel at their relationship. Seeing them together brings to mind often the good memories of Dad and me (before he bought the bar).

Yes, Mickey Pond — now, there's another hundred pages. He plays only one song, LAT 44, on his guitar and amp in the barn not far from the front of the house. His song changes as Prairieville does, with unpredictable spacings between the notes that are always changing. I can't tell you how good it sounds, for I am no expert at music. But it sure sounds good to me.

Then there are Katie and Johnny, two young people that Mr. P is very fond of. He calls Katie a "flapper" — a creative dresser with an eye for style and fashion. Mr. P has told me more than once that she will be designing clothes one day. I've seen the confidence and joy she gets from making things for people, and it's all so wonderful to see.

Johnny Apple has flown his model airplanes here since he was a little boy, beginning with a hand-held chuck glider made of balsa wood. He'd throw it from atop the seventy-foot cliff line of quartzite rock. Now Johnny is a licensed pilot and recently flew over Prairieville to scatter his father's ashes on this land where his father worked as a caretaker. Johnny's alcoholic father killed himself not long ago. I won't go into the details; but as you can imagine, it was awful.

I was in the barn the other day listening to LAT 44 when Johnny came by. He talked about a girl he met at the airfield where he works. I envied him, for I haven't felt that way about a girl since Lauren. Often I think of Lauren in San Diego. I wonder if she is married and has children and what her life is like now. I'm not sure why I never stayed in touch with her and often resist the temptation to try and reach her by phone. Oh, well ... I'm lamenting days gone by, and that's a pathetic way of being.

143

In closing, I hope your health is well, Mother. And Sara, my best to you and Tim, and hugs and kisses for those two little rascal nephews of mine.

I will write more later about my summer at Prairieville.

> *Love,*
>
> *Eddie*

Upon addressing his letter, he looked out his bedroom window and saw Katie and Johnny walking down the lane on their way to the barn where Mickey was still busy scraping paint.

Johnny had been talking to Katie about Hanna and how he wanted to invite her to one of Mr. P's barbeques. "I can fly one of my radio-controlled planes from the cliff line while Mickey blasts LAT 44 over the airwaves."

Katie was happy for Johnny and yet had a girl's crush on him. However, she knew that after losing his father in such a terrible way, this was good for him.

They also talked about their first session with Dr. Wertz, a female psychologist whom they both liked. When leaving the Spink house, Johnny asked Katie, "Did anything come up for you? I mean, last night I had this crazy dream about my dad. He was flying one of my planes with me at Prairieville ... then he was my copilot in a jet I was flying over water. I don't ever remember having a dream about my dad."

"You'll have to tell Dr. Wertz about it. She said she wanted me to pay attention to my dreams. I haven't dreamed about my mother yet ... but maybe I will. Oh! One thing! I find myself thinking or remembering good memories of her. Like when she'd take me shopping for clothes at the mall ... or when we sunbathed together in our backyard in Lemon before we moved here." She paused reflectively for a moment, then asked, "How's your mom doing?"

"She's busy ironing all the time ... day and night. Thanks to Mr. P sending her my dad's check every week, she doesn't have to work as hard as she does. But people keep bringing their clothes to her by the carload."

"Well, at least she's busy ... and that's good.

"Yeah."

Eighteen-year-old Hanna Storm's nickname was Stormy. Her father called her that ever since she was a little girl when she'd have fierce temper tantrums in order to get the attention she craved. The curly-haired brunette was homecoming queen her senior year at Marshall High and certainly had her share of boyfriends. She wasn't sure if she liked Johnny in that way, mainly because she thought he was too short for her slender five-foot-seven frame.

Johnny invited Hanna to Mr. P's afternoon Fourth of July barbeque with a fireworks show after dark from the cliff line. Mickey and Eddie went to South Dakota and bought fireworks at a stand a couple of miles from the Minnesota border.

Katie and Karl arrived early to help Mr. P set up for their meal of grilled burgers and hot dogs. Katie brought a fruit salad that she and her dad had made together.

It was hot all day with clear skies and very little wind, which was unusual any time of the year at Prairieville. Mr. P was feeling fit — better than he had in years. His exercise regimen with Eddie was giving him the energy he needed for a quality life in his "golden years."

Johnny brought his date in Mr. P's truck. Katie was impressed with Hanna, admiring her taste in clothes. At first she thought Hanna was too pretty for Johnny, but then she dismissed the notion upon seeing how happy Johnny seemed with Hanna there.

On the back deck while drinking lemonade, Hanna told Katie, "I just love the color of your hair."

"Thank you," Katie replied. "My mother had the same color when she was young."

"Johnny told me your mother passed away. I'm so sorry, Katie."

"Oh, it's okay. We were never really close."

"I know what that's like ... My mother and I fight all the time."

"Really? About what?"

"Stupid things ... that aren't worth mentioning."

On the way home with the fireworks in Mickey's Durango, Mickey and Eddie talked about their first sessions with the therapist. They both agreed that Dr. Wertz could help them move on to live better lives.

"I told her I want to move my music to another level ... to a higher frequency ... and she totally got it. It was so cool. I told her I put my heart into my music and expected it to be, at the very least, 'real.' And she totally got that too! Right away after my session ... when you were in your session with her ... I started feeling the anger I had for Ned and Bert when I lived on the farm. It was so real how bored I was all the time from living with those two stiffs. The same meals for eighteen years ... a menu of big-time resentment. I used to throw up Bert's food upstairs in my bathroom after just about every meal. That's why I was such a bean pole."

"You have gained some weight at Prairieville," Eddie observed.

"Yeah! About twenty pounds! And my acne cleared up. That's the best thing. I had pimples all the time ever since I was thirteen. I think the well water on the farm was loaded with pesticides and toxins from animal crap. Ever since I started drinking my dad's bottled water, I haven't had many pimples at all. What did you get from your session, Eddie?"

"Oh, let me see ... I talked about my family and my ex-girlfriend, Lauren."

"Lauren, huh? What was she like?"

"She was a natural beauty ... and one of those free spirits that only seem to be in California. She was older than me ... like in her mid-twenties when I was eighteen ... nineteen. She helped me get my book published. Her father was a printer in San Francisco. I don't think I could've ever published my book if not for them."

"How come you didn't stay together?"

"I was jealous of her independence. I was selling my book and we separated ... as friends."

"And you never saw her or talked to her again?"

"We got together in Oklahoma for a lost weekend once. Long story short, I was on a ferry crossing this gargantuan lake in Oklahoma soon after I last saw Lauren. A storm came and my van and I were tossed off the ferry to the bottom of that lake."

"Wow! You were inside your van at the bottom of a lake?"

"Yeah."

"How'd you get out?"

I broke a window, and I passed out as I floated to the surface on a foam mattress. All I can tell you is I had the longest and strangest dream when I was floating on that lake."

"What was the dream about?"

I was in this coma for years. When I came out of the coma in my dream ... I had a son who was about your age ..."

"Was he your son from that weekend with Lauren?"

"Yeah. Anyway, his name was Les Dense."

"Sweet! That's what I want my music to be ... less dense."

"Exactly! When I woke up from that dream on the shore of that lake, I was less dense. I could see things so clearly. I was really present ... alive."

"That's so cool! You are more present than anybody I know."

"Well ... it didn't go away ... even though I pretty much shut down writing, and I lived with my folks in one big, boring existence. I bartended in my parents' bar for several years, and then I spent many more years driving a cab.

"How did you stay ... less dense?"

"I don't know. I just did. I think it was because I had a near-death experience ... and it woke me up."

"Sweet. That's what I want my music to do ... wake me up ... so I can reach higher levels of playing."

When they returned home, they stopped on the Prairieville lane and took the fireworks up the path that led to the cliff line. From atop the cliff line, Mickey could see one of Johnny's model planes with his kit on the bed of his dad's old truck. He was looking forward to seeing his friend and meeting his new girlfriend, Hanna. Both he and Johnny were not interested in any of the girls in their small graduation class. This girl from Marshall who also flew real airplanes might have a girlfriend Mickey could meet, and perhaps they could double-date. Johnny was cool with the idea about setting up Mickey. Hanna wanted to meet Mickey first, however, to size him up and match him up with the right friend.

Wallis and Karl had the burgers and dogs ready, and they all self-served and ate their food on the back deck. Johnny introduced Hanna to Mickey.

"So you're the famous Mickey Pond," she smiled as she shook his hand.

"Famous? Famous for what?" Mickey smiled back.

"I hear you're quite the musician and that we may get to hear your song ... What's it called?"

"LAT 44," Johnny interjected. "Will you play after we eat?" he asked his friend.

"Yeah ... I guess."

Katie told Johnny's girlfriend that Mickey was her half-brother — that they had the same mother.

"That explains why you have the same color hair," Hanna remarked.

Hanna Storm had a carefree manner about her, and she noticed everything. Mickey could see Johnny watching Hanna's every glance and hanging on every word she spoke. It was as if this girl had done something to his friend that was inexplicable. Her words were extensive and too polished, as was evident when she was introduced to Mr. P. She was respectful when she mentioned his flying exploits. "My father has talked about you to other pilots, that you were one of the pioneers of aviation."

Of course Wallis liked the confident young woman and had good things to say about her father. "Yes, I remember seeing your father around the airfield. He was such a precocious young man," Pond recalled with such joy that the whole gathering smiled and laughed markedly.

"I would love to see Superland," Hanna expressed with such genuine animation that Johnny offered to show her the vintage plane after wolfing down his burger.

When Johnny turned on the light above Superland, Hanna approached it with reverence as her date removed the tarp covering it. He watched her peering inside the dark cockpit and breathing in the smells of the old leather seat while staring at the primitive gauges.

She wanted to sit in the pilot's seat, and Johnny quickly accommodated. It was then he discovered Pond's secret compartment, opened it, and found the stowed copy of Mr. P's last book. He closed the secret compartment, leaving *Superland* where he found it and not telling his date what he had found.

Mickey and Katie came into the barn and found Johnny talking to Hanna, who was in the pilot's seat. Mickey turned on a light by the workbench and flipped on his amp. LAT 44 began with his black pick warming up each string. Hanna hushed Johnny's talk with her finger to her lips so that she could hear Mickey's song. For twenty minutes Hanna listened with all her senses taking in the nerve-tingling notes that moved all over the musical scale of sound's possibilities.

The artist with his guitar lost himself in a song that even Johnny had not heard him play as well as now. Johnny became jealous of Hanna's brown eyes that were closed in order to shut out anything visual. He thought the song would never end. And when it did, the storm inside his belly churned with the awareness that men become talented at something for the love of women.

His date lavished praise on the artist. Words like "amazing" and "incredible." "I was mesmerized," she confessed to Johnny as he stewed with his jealous storm within.

Suddenly his friend from Madisonville who came here with nothing in a stolen car was now a godlike musician who was also lucky to be rich like Hanna.

The fireworks display from the cliff line was the last straw for Johnny as Hanna stood atop the cliff line with Mickey lighting the flares and rockets over Prairieville while Johnny watched from Mr. P's truck. He was so upset that he didn't fly his plane for her. He told her the wind wasn't right, which was a lie.

Driving Hanna home later that night, she talked on and on about Mickey's music and how any of her girlfriends would adore him. When she got out of the truck, he just drove away without any plans for a double date. He scoffed inwardly, *She's not my type,* and headed home.

* * * * *

The barn was painted by late July, and Mickey had two more weeks before he left for Ireland for ten days. A healthier Wallis Pond was delighted with his son's work and put him to work cleaning the basement and cutting firewood for the coming winter.

Johnny hadn't been over to Prairieville to visit Mickey since the Fourth of July barbeque. Hanna was out of the picture now after Johnny declined two of her offers to fix Mickey up with one of her friends on a double date.

After working at the airfield, Johnny came by in the truck to pick up Mr. P's garbage. The manuscript he'd found in Superland's secret compartment had been on his mind. Before hauling the garbage to the dump, he parked in front of the barn and removed the copy of the book from its hiding place. His plan was to read it fast and return it before anyone knew it was missing.

He began reading it in his room when he returned home from the county dump. From the very beginning the story held his attention, mostly because of the flying Billy did. He thought the book would help him forget Hanna and the terrible ordeal of finding his father dead in the bar.

On his fifth night of reading, he came to several accounts in the book about the relationship between Marilyn Spink and his father. He was certain the book played a part in his father's decision to end his life.

The thought of having *Superland* published didn't agree with Johnny, mostly because his mother would be hurt by her husband's infidelity. It took him three more days to return the book to its hiding place inside the vintage plane he would inherit when Mr. P died.

Upon returning the last book, he decided to visit Mickey, who was in his room reading a travel guide about Ireland. It wasn't the old man's book that he wanted to discuss, because he had read it like a spy — the way his father might have read it, for all he knew. There was something else. Hanna. A couple weeks ago in the hangar at the airfield, she said she wanted Mickey to play at a party she was having at her house the coming weekend. She had invited Johnny to her party; he said he wasn't sure he cold make it, but he would ask Mickey. Now he was feeling guilty about not telling Mickey about the gig, and he wanted to unload his feelings he'd kept inside ever since the barbeque.

"Did Hanna call you about playing at her party this weekend?" the young pilot asked the young musician.

"No. What party?"

"Her birthday party. She asked me to give you her number to call her about it."

After Johnny wrote down Hanna's phone number and gave it to Mickey, Johnny asked him if he was going to call her.

"I don't' know. I only know one song. I can't play just one song for twenty minutes," he thought out loud.

"Why not? It's a good song. They'll love it."

"Uh ... I don't think it would work."

"Well ... will ya call her and let her know?"

"Yeah ... I guess."

After an awkward silence Johnny added, "You know, when you played at the Fourth of July barbeque?"

"Yeah."

"All the way home that night she raved about your playing ... and how she would line you up with her friends and we could double date."

"Really?"

"Yeah. But I was jealous. I turned her down when she wanted us to all go out."

Mickey's eyes asked him why.

"I was jealous of your talent, Mickey. I'm sorry. I didn't want to compete with you. I know that's stupid, but I had to tell ya." Johnny paused and looked at the floor for a minute, then he looked back at Mickey. "I found your dad's last book in Superland when I was showing it to Hanna that day. I took it and read it."

"Really?"

"Yeah ... but don't tell your dad."

"Don't worry ... I won't."

"See ... there's some bad stuff in the book about my dad and your mom. My dad was spying for her while he worked here, and Mr. P knew it all along. I don't want to believe the stuff my dad did, but Mr. P isn't a mean person ... And my dad ... well, he had his problems. Mr. P has been so good to me and my mom ... I guess I told you because I don't want to be like my dad."

"You should tell my dad you read it. I don't think he'd mind at all if you read it. I plan on reading it after I finish his other books."

"It's a good story."

"Are you worried he'll publish it?" Mickey asked.

"Only for my mom's sake."

"I think Eddie was going to sell it to my dad's readers when he first came here ... but I don't know if he still is. Eddie's writing his second book now. You should tell him what you told me. You know how Eddie is. He listens to people and wouldn't sell the book if it'd hurt someone."

"Yeah, I know. But don't talk to Eddie about it. I'll talk to him."

"Yeah ... sure. And you know that my dad's leaving me the rights to all his books. I would never publish it. No way ... I don't need to."

"Thanks, Mickey. So you're really going to Ireland?"

"Yeah. I got my passport and reservation."

"Cool. What're ya gonna do over there?"

"I'm gonna go all over the country."

"What made ya want to go there?"

"My dad's Irish ... on his dad's side. I read that in his books. And it just made me want to go there."

"Sweet."

On his way home Johnny felt better after telling Mickey how he felt about the book and Hanna's party invitation. Yet while leaving on the lane to Prairieville, he felt like the son of an intruder. The son of a spy. The son of Mr. P's twisted caretaker who betrayed his generous boss.

Driving slowly down Kenwick Road, he recalled reading in *Superland* how his father was fired for drinking on the job when he worked for the county as a garbage man. Despite that, Mr. P hired his father right away and paid his high insurance premiums so he could continue driving for him. "What a jerk you were, Dad," he muttered while parking in the Apple driveway.

Later that night as he was lying on his bed, relieved to have talked to his friend and to have returned the manuscript to its hiding place, he thought of Mr. P's last book and how Billy Lake wanted a "different" life for the son he never knew. Yet Billy struggled with the very same issues his parents had passed on to him. He wrote about the "vicious circle of same" — how difficult it is to be different from your parents.

Johnny tightened his fists at his sides and pounded them onto his mattress, swearing out loud, "I will NOT be like my father." Low self-esteem and jealousy were traits his father had passed on to him. "I am a licensed pilot. I have done things with my life already that he was afraid to do. I will be DIFFERENT from him," he swore to the dark ceiling.

Before sleep came he took his mind to flying — the one thing he knew well and the one thing that relaxed him. He remembered Wade telling him, "You have an advanced feel for flying ... able to adjust your aircraft in precarious winds without hesitation."

Johnny was aware that even his talent for flying he owed to Mr. P. Countless times the old aviator had come outside to give him tips and praise and welcome corrections after watching him fly from his cliff line. And now he realized that it was Mr. P he was flying for. The one person who motivated him to be better and better — to be different.

When Mickey called Hanna it was just two days before her party. She begged him to play for her nineteenth birthday. His intention was to decline, but he gave in and said he would be there at nine o'clock and play for twenty minutes.

He stared down at the directions to her house that she'd given him. She sounded too sweet — as if she really liked him. Over and over her sweet words kept coming back to him. "I want to be your first ... performance ... and will pay you fifty dollars for it," she'd giggled sensuously.

Mickey knew no way to respond to that hidden meaning from an attractive girl like Hanna. Never had he kissed a girl, and this was the girl Johnny liked — or had liked. *What would I do?* he worried.

The next day he talked to Eddie about his dilemma. "My intention was to decline playing for the party, but instead I ended up committing to it. I don't want to hurt Johnny by playing at Hanna's party."

"It doesn't hurt to have fun, Mickey. To be paid for your art doesn't hurt anybody and can empower you to new levels."

"That's what I want."

"And girls love artists. At least some girls do."

"Did girls like you because you're an artist?"

"Not many," Eddie laughed. "But one girl did."

"Lauren?"

"Yeah. I often thought that men create things for the love of women. It's a natural thing. If not for women ... men would live in caves. Just be Mickey Pond. Play your music ... and see what happens. You won't do anything you don't want to do ... But that doesn't mean you won't regret it later."

"That's what I'm worried about. Later," Mickey said.

The Storm home was a twenty-room, brick, ranch-style house in the country north of Marshall. Situated alone atop a hill, Mickey wasn't sure he was at the right house until he saw Storm on the mailbox on the service road in front of it. There were perhaps three dozen vehicles parked on the graveled, up-sloping drive. They were the expensive vehicles of the wealthy youth around Marshall. Mickey didn't know what Hanna's father did; but whatever it was, it was certainly prosperous.

He carried his guitar and amp up toward an open, lit, four-stall garage. The frenetic party chatter of what sounded like at least a hundred people came from the other side of the house. It suddenly dawned on Mickey that he may get paranoid with stage fright since he'd never played for a large group of strangers before. He scanned over the parked vehicles hoping to see his dad's old truck. It wasn't there.

He leaned his guitar case next to his amp just inside the garage against a corner wall, then he walked over to a gazebo that was about fifty yards away from the house. This was a time to meditate — to quiet his busy mind like Eddie had taught him to do. He sat on a hard-cushioned seat in the gazebo with his forearms resting on his thighs. As he closed his eyes, he followed each deep breath, paying close attention to the gaps between each inhalation and exhalation. Again and again he dismissed each anxious thought until the space between them grew longer and longer.

Eddie had told him, "When your mind is thinking about clock time or how long you've been sitting, say 'I' to yourself when you inhale and 'am' when you exhale."

After repeating the "I am" mantra for what seemed like a hundred times, Mickey opened his eyes and looked around. He felt relaxed and ready to meet the party. He thought about what Eddie said to him when he left the house. "When you are around people who are drinking, appearing to be having a good time, you will pick up negative energy and waves of fear. Do not think it's your fear. It's theirs. Do not own it. Let it pass through you and be Mickey Pond. Now go play for you. Play your LAT 44 and know that you are responsible for dismissing all fear around you and making a better space for all."

He stood up and walked across the manicured lawn toward the other side of the house. He saw a large gathering of casually dressed people his age mingling on an elevated, spacious redwood deck. Purple glow lamps that killed mosquitoes were lit on each corner of the deck and cast a soft violet shade on all of the faces and uncovered skin.

Wearing his black jeans with black sleeveless T-shirt and black Nikes, he glanced down at his red hammer while standing under one of the purple lights. He saw that his tattoo was blood red, and his arms were bigger from splitting so much wood.

The guests on the deck were friendly, nodding hello while holding their drinks as he passed. All were strangers to him, these people he would soon play for, and he liked their energy.

He made his way into the crowded house that was decorated with expensive balloons and streamers. A banner over the fireplace read "HAPPY BIRTHDAY HANNA." On the other side of the large room he saw Hanna chatting and laughing with a few of her guests. She looked beautiful to him. Her dark-brown hair was cut shorter and styled differently than when he saw her at the barbeque. Something else was different too. She was wearing red lipstick that made her teeth look whiter.

It was not Mickey's style to wave at her to catch her eye in the crowd. He had to go over to her. Her back was to him as he approached. She was wearing a green halter top with frayed denim cutoff shorts and sandals. She held a mixed drink in her hand with expensive rings on her fingers. He could hear her laughter more as he stood ten feet from her. For some reason she turned and saw him.

"Mickey!" she screamed and walked over to him. "Thank you so much for coming!" Her brown eyes were big and clear and direct into his gray eyes. "Can I get you something to drink?"

"Yeah ... a Coke or something."

"You mean something with Coke ... like bourbon or Jack Daniels?"

"No. I don't drink alcohol."

"Is Johnny with you?" she asked.

"No ... he isn't here?"

"I invited him. I haven't seen him. I'll get ya a Coke. Be right back."

He watched her go into the kitchen and hoped he could set up and play on the deck. He knew the sound would carry better outside. There were lots of pretty girls at the party — quite a difference compared to Kenwick and LeRoy.

When Hanna returned with his Coke, she brought along a pretty girlfriend and introduced her to him. "Mickey, this is Amber," Hanna giggled.

Amber shook Mickey's hand and said, "I'm pleased to meet you."

"Mickey's going to play his guitar for us. You will be impressed, Amber. Believe me," Hanna raved.

"Can I play on the deck?"

"Sure ... there's plenty of outlets. My dad's an electrical engineer," she laughed.

"When do you want me to play?"

"Whenever you're ready."

"I'll go get my stuff," he said as he started for the door.

"Can I help?" Hanna asked.

"No ... I can do it."

He left the way he came in and brought his guitar and amp back up to the deck. The guests on the deck made room for Mickey and were buzzing around the entertainment to come. He turned on his guitar and cranked up his amp volume to the max. Perhaps his guests were not expecting much from a one-man band, but that soon changed when LAT 44 began on the deck of the Storm house. Mickey filled the summer night airwaves with such incredible sounds that more and more people came out of the house to hear it and see who was playing this music.

Hanna came out with Amber, and they stood mesmerized with the others — in awe of the sounds that came from the tall, skinny kid with brindle-colored hair. His eyes were closed and locked into his creative genius that was generated by the black pick he moved so fast at times that it appeared invisible.

LAT 44 never sounded better — or more different, moving its listeners to ineffable emotions that rose and fell between the gaps of Mickey's strings. At times he played the love of his father and how he had given him his new life in Prairieville. Then he played the exhilarating flights of Johnny Apple on the cliff line and Lucky soaring free in Yankton. Then Katie, his sweet sister who adored her father and mourned the selfish mother they shared. Then Eddie, the mystery man who appeared out of nowhere and was there for all of them when they needed a mentor. He was a friend who had reached this same frequency Mickey now had. He finished his haunting song with his mother — notes as if she were out there, yet she was behind the artist's closed eyes, swimming in the inky darkness of the prairie. Yes, these were the waves of notes riding forgiveness as if she were here now, out there in the audience that was feeling and trembling with him. They felt his ten thousand days and nights of aloneness on the farm. He ended his song with Lloyd Apple's swaying basement shadow that his son would have to overcome with the same forgiveness. Just as he had done with an absent father who finally showed him that he wanted to be his father.

There was no raucous applause from alcohol when LAT 44 stopped, only silence. He had achieved the gap in frequency he had aimed for. They weren't sure he had finished until he opened his eyes and could see them all agape, unable to applaud because of the drink they forgot was there. Then all at once they set down their drinks and morphed into one body of thundering applause.

He nodded once at them and mouthed "thank you" before unplugging his black instrument and returning it to its case.

Hanna came up to him and kissed his neck, thanking him for playing and telling him it was the best part of her birthday. Standing on the deck he could smell her sweet perfume and the clean smell of her hair. He could see clearly why his friend liked this girl who was out of his league — and Mickey's.

She begged him to stay for a late movie on their big-screen TV. "Everyone will be gone ... except for me and Amber." The thought of being around two attractive girls intimidated him, so he declined her invitation politely, telling her he had to get up early for work.

She walked with him to his Durango and insisted on carrying his guitar case. Whatever she said on the way to the Durango was lost in the way she walked close to him. Her soft, bare arm touched against his arm as they made their way down the lush lawn to his vehicle.

"I wish you could stay," she lamented, then hugged him around his lower back. She pressed her chest against his heart which made it beat faster, as if he were frightened. "I hope I can see you again ... soon," she waved coyly and watched him drive away.

He drove in a dazed state of arousal all the way to Kenwick with her sweet perfume yet in his nostrils. As much as he knew about the dating game, he did know that Johnny was better looking than he, and that Hanna was attracted to LAT 44, not him physically.

Back home Mr. P and Eddie asked him all about his first gig. It was his dad that noticed the red lipstick on his neck. "Looks like she really liked your performance," he laughed when pointing out the red mark.

"She kissed me," he said defensively.

"I can see that," Pond chuckled.

"We're just friends," Mickey added.

"It's best to start out that way," his father smiled.

* * * * *

Ten days after her party, Hanna surprised Mickey by stopping by Prairieville to pay him fifty bucks for playing at her party. He was stacking firewood in the barn when she parked her new red Volvo in front of the open barn door. As she handed him the cash, she apologized for forgetting to pay him. "But at least it gave me a chance to see you again before I go off to college in Mankato. I want to be a teacher," she smiled.

"That's good," he nodded shyly then wiped the sweat from his face with an oil rag. He offered her some lemonade from a big pitcher his dad had brought out to him earlier. Like Mickey, she drank straight from the pitcher.

"Boy, that's good!" she laughed.

"My dad made it."

After an awkward pause, she told him she'd be in Mankato by the time he returned from Ireland. She gave him her cell number and said, "Call me as soon as you get back. I want to hear all about your trip."

"Okay," he courtesy smiled.

Johnny had his plane in the back of Mr. P's truck to fly it from the cliff line and was on his way to Prairieville when he spotted Hanna's car parked by the barn. Instead of going up to the cliff line, he turned around and headed back down the lane, not wanting to run into Hanna. His jealous mind kept telling him that she and Mickey were now dating after he played at her party. When he saw Hanna at the airfield the day before, she went on an on to him about how Mickey played his "incredible music" at her party, and she wished he would have been there to hear it.

As a result of his encounter with Hanna, Johnny had come to Prairieville to fly and find out how the gig went. But most of all, he wanted to find out if Mickey liked Hanna. Now it was obvious to Johnny that Hanna liked Mickey because she drove all the way out to Prairieville to see him.

All the way home Johnny listened to his jealous thoughts of Mickey and Hanna, and he realized he'd have to talk about them to his therapist. He and Katie were going the next afternoon for their scheduled sessions.

Hanna hung around the barn long enough to see that Mickey was not going to ask her out on a date before he left for Ireland. He consciously kept his sweaty body away from one of her potential hugs, so she left reminding him to call her when he got back from his trip.

That evening just before going to bed, Wallis complained to Eddie of chest pains. Eddie played it safe and drove him to an outpatient heart clinic in Dakota Falls, and Mickey rode along. Wallis was admitted after tests confirmed he'd had a mild heart attack. On the drive to the hospital, the tired old man said he'd had his previous two strokes in August. Eddie asked him if there was any event in his life that happened in August, but Wallis said he couldn't think of anything "significant."

Mickey was worried about his father — so much so that he canceled his refundable flight to Ireland. He told Eddie, "I would only worry about him over there. I can always go later."

Wallis was in the hospital for five days. He was waiting in his chair, ready to go home, when Eddie and Mickey came to get him on the day his doctor released him. He had told his frustrated doctor the day before, "I'm too old for heart surgery. I wanna die in my own bed at Prairieville."

On Sunday Mickey told his bed-resting father that he'd canceled his trip. Pond was disappointed for his son, telling him, "You should see the world whether I'm dead or alive."

Eddie was in the throes of his second novel when Mickey knocked on his bedroom door after taking his father a cup of hot black tea with lemon and honey. "I'm worried about my dad. He appears to be weaker since he came home from the hospital."

"I know. It seems as if he's at peace with his life and ready to let go of the world."

"Isn't there something that can be done?" Mickey pleaded with Eddie.

"He won't have surgery. You know that. He's lived a long, hard life ... and he might be ready to leave it soon."

"I haven't read all his books yet, and I'd like to read the last one. Should I ask him if I can read it?"

"You can if you want. I'm sure he'd want you to read it."

"Can you get it for me?"

"Sure."

All afternoon and late into the night, Mickey read *Superland* in his room until he had finished it. He could see why Johnny didn't want it published for his mother's sake, and he told Eddie just that when he returned the manuscript to him the next morning.

Wallis had made it clear that he wanted Eddie to stay at Prairieville when he passed away. He wanted Eddie to take his place as a mentor for his son when he was gone. For the two hundred thousand Pond had deposited into Eddie's checking account, Eddie wondered how long he would be obligated to stay there. *Could I leave Prairieville after only another year?* he pondered, knowing his second book would be finished by then. *Would Mr. P's loyal readers even be interested in my book?*

Eddie didn't have to wait long to get the answers to his questions. The next day when Mickey was mowing the lawn around the house, Eddie went into the old man's bedroom. It was right after his concerned nurse had informed Eddie of her patient's higher blood pressure and increased heart rate.

Pond was staring out his bedroom window, watching for whenever his son would pass by his window on his green John Deere lawnmower that Lloyd Apple had kept in top running condition.

"Mr. P, could I talk with you about a few things?"

"Yes ... as long as it's not about heart surgery," Pond scoffed.

"No ... no, it's about other things."

"I'm listening."

"You've read *Blue River* and you've seen how my writing style compares to yours. Do you think your readers would be a plausible market for my books?"

"While there is much in our writing styles that is very different, Mr. Dense, there is also much that is very similar. Your book will certainly be different than mine, but I think you'll find my loyal readers to be a good market for your books."

"And you haven't changed your mind about my using your list and your route to market my book to your readers?"

"No, I don't have a problem with that. Ultimately, though, it's up to Mickey. The list is his. It's in my safe deposit box, and my executor will give it to him upon my death."

"Okay. Now, about the money you gave me ... I may use some of it to publish my book. But how long would you expect me to stay on at Prairieville when you're gone? I mean ... I would want to see that Mickey has my support until he could live here alone, but how long ..."

"Eddie ... Eddie ... I don't want any time restrictions put on your life. I would've published *Superland* by now and paid someone to market it to my readers if Mickey hadn't come here. I know you came here because of that offer in my letter ... and I

162

have no qualms about anything you do or how long you stay." After a brief pause Wallis added, "Tell me something ... I read your first book. What is your second book about ... without giving away too much or diminishing your storyline?"

"Well ... I've written some eighty pages of the first draft. So far it's about Prairieville. Mickey and Johnny are in it. Mickey plays his guitar and Johnny flies his planes from the cliff line. Katie is a young girl who has to choose between her brother and the young pilot when ..."

"Is there a crusty old man living at Prairieville?" Pond chuckled and coughed.

"Yes," Eddie smiled.

"What does Katie choose?" the old author asked as his creative eyes twinkled.

"I don't know yet ... but yet I know I want them to become conscious ... different ... to make this world a better place, if you will."

"Do these characters have to suffer to reach this consciousness? Must there not be conflict and pain?"

"That's why it's different. And that's the toughest part of making their rise to consciousness credible, Mr. P ... reaching it by their own desire to reach a higher frequency of aliveness. In my own recent therapy sessions, I've become aware of my own desire to create a new world for myself by self-abnegation ... denying my own worldly pleasures of America's concept of the happy family in the big house with material needs met. I've resisted the normal life because 'normal' in America has reached a level of insanity that only intensifies when I try to join the herd."

"I see. So you want to live a different way ... away from the herd?"

"Yes. Yet I must write for the herd. My job is to not strengthen the herd ... to make it stronger by diminishing their numbers."

"That sounds interesting, Eddie," Pond coughed. "I always wrote for me ... to resolve my own petty life through Billy Lake. It's a selfish way to write. You at least want positive change. I wish you well with it."

"Thank you. But I can't help but feel that your books were not 'selfish.' You wanted your readers to know your life as it truly was. I have not lived but a fraction of your difficult journey ... And if I had lived your life, I doubt that I would have had the courage to write about it so beautifully.

"Inasmuch as I appreciate your kind words ... I have had my share of regrets about the way I've lived my life ..." Pond turned his head to the window in order to see Mickey pass by until he was out of sight. "That's my biggest regret," he admitted upon turning back to Eddie. "To have him in my life for only a short time ... Oh, I could be positive and say I'm thankful for all the time I've had with him ... and I am. Yet it's those eighteen years without him that have weakened my heart to this point. The damage has been done ... and I regret that. I can't help it. I just do.

"Yes, I understand, Mr. P. I understand."

"I know you do," the old man sighed and extended his trembling hand for Eddie to take, and they clasped hands tightly. "I want you to live your life, Eddie Dense, without that kind of regret."

"I will," Eddie smiled down at his favorite writer. He watched him as his son passed by another time.

He's Gone

By the 7th of September, Pond's nurse was staying overnight at Prairieville in order to make her beloved patient as comfortable as possible in his final days.

Mickey was at his father's bedside when he died. With a face splashed with tears he told him, "I always loved you."

The dying man nodded as if he knew exactly what his son meant, for he too had always loved his own father.

Eddie's last visit with Wallis was much less dramatic, both knowing in each man's eyes that death meant inner peace for a man who had lived his life to the best of his ability.

"He's gone," his nurse said softly upon checking his pulse.

Mickey went out to the barn and removed the canvas tarp covering Superland. He climbed into the pilot's seat and cried for the loss of a father he had come to know and love.

Indian summer came when Mickey released his father's ashes from the cliff line with Johnny, Katie and Eddie by his side. Pond's executor, Mrs. Thistlethwaite, his nurse, Karl, and Maxine all stood near the front of the house during the private ceremony.

Later that day as they sat around the dining room table, the executor read the will. There were no big surprises, except Wallis arranged for his estate to pay for the kids' therapy, and Johnny had been given unlimited credit at the airfield.

After the reading of the will, Mickey gave Katie a copy of *Superland* to read, since she was the only one who hadn't read it. "I think you should read this," he told his sister. "There's things in there about Mom and Lloyd Apple you should know."

"Has Johnny read it?"

Mickey nodded yes.

"What did he say?"

"Mostly that he didn't want it published for his mother's sake. I can understand that. It doesn't need to be published. My dad left it up to me ... and I don't see any reason to. You don't have to read it if you don't want to."

"No ... I want to."

Katie and Karl left and only Johnny remained after Maxine drove herself home in her car. Johnny was elated that now he could fly more hours and now had a chance for a good job with a company that would pay for his jet training. And Johnny had gotten over his jealousy about Hanna liking Mickey ever since she left for college in Mankato. He admitted that he envied Mickey's creative talent. "You'll get girls like crazy," he told the budding musician.

"You can fly! And I'd say that's gonna be more than most guys can say. Besides, I don't want a girl who likes me for what I do. I want a girl who truly sees me."

"Aw, Mickey ... it's like Mr. P used to say to us. Everything boys and men do is for the love of a female. I know I fly 'cause I like to ... but I have to admit he was right. Don't you think?"

"I can't say. I know Hanna likes me for my music ... And I think 'cause I know that ... I wasn't really interested in her."

"She's outta my league. But not yours. You're rich."

"My dad said to watch out for the girls who want ya ... 'cause they see somethin' they want that you can't see."

"I don't know what that means," Johnny said.

"He said that women run the world. And until you respect that, you'll always be run by them."

"Is that why he never got married?"

"I guess he wanted to run his own life. And that's not a bad thing."

"Yeah," Johnny agreed.

"I mean ... in his books he wrote about these women in his life until he saw some 'thing' in each one that turned him away from them. He'd always end it with each one ... before they knew anything was wrong."

"But he kept my dad and your mother in his life even though they betrayed him," Johnny said.

"I think that was because of us and Katie."

"Yeah," Johnny agreed. "It's like ... I mean, after reading *Superland* ... he wanted our lives to be different than his life." Johnny looked into the gray eyes of Wallis Pond's son and asked him, "What do we do now that he's gone?"

Mickey didn't know what to say until he thought about what his father wanted from him. "Like you said, I think he wants us to be different ... like he was, but without the hardships he went through."

"Yeah," Johnny agreed solemnly with a positive nod.

"I gave Katie *Superland* to read. She wanted to read it."

Johnny nodded and realized out loud, "I still have my mom and Katie and Karl. It's like your dad brought Eddie here to somehow take his place."

Mickey agreed with his nod and added, "I still have my music."

"That's true."

When Johnny left Prairieville, it was Mickey and Eddie alone in the big house for the first time. They each looked around the living room and saw the things that reminded them of Wallis Pond — the blackened fireplace he used all winter, the rows of stacked books along the wall that nourished his mind and soul, his cluttered desk that smelled of old pipe tobacco from his smoking days of old, and his parked chair at his desk that gave him legs to move about his beloved Prairieville.

"He wanted me to give his chair to the nursing home in LeRoy," Eddie said softly.

"I'll take it there," Mickey said.

"Now?"

"Yeah."

"I'll go with you."

They loaded the chair into the Durango and drove away from Prairieville on what appeared to be the first day of autumn. Cool breezes blew and swirled into the deep grasses of summer's yield. A red-tailed hawk floated over its airspace, playing in the winds as if being watched by an old spirit who lived there for many years.

Within a week of Pond's death, his executor had all of his client's bequests and affairs in order. Mickey Pond was officially a wealthy young man with control over all of his father's vast estate and assets. One thing Mr. P forgot to do was sign over the title to his old truck to Johnny Apple, so Mickey did that right away. Then he called his friend and told him the truck was his.

Johnny was surprised and grateful, informing his friend that he would continue hauling his garbage from Prairieville every two weeks at no charge. Mickey also reminded Johnny that Superland was his now, and that he could store it in the barn, sell it, or take it whenever he wanted. Johnny said that Wade Hampton had offered him thirty thousand for it, so Johnny said he wanted to check out the plane's value to see whether he should sell it or hold onto the vintage aircraft.

Mickey had no plans for his future. Even Ireland was on the back burner until he got used to his new life on "his" Prairieville. He hadn't felt like playing his music ever since his father died, but he was now ready to go to the barn, pick up his guitar, and assault the airwaves.

Eddie could hear LAT 44 from inside the house, and again he was amazed how the sounds had morphed to fit the loss of his father. Eddie was so impressed that he could easily imagine the song on a CD and marketed to a vast audience. *Perhaps that is why I'm here,* he mused, *to help him launch his music into the universe.*

Mickey and Eddie began to sort through Wallis's vast library, donating the books neither wanted to the LeRoy Public Library. At first Mickey wanted to read every book his father had collected, but then upon further examination he thought some of the titles were of such boring content that he knew he would never even begin to read them.

Eventually Eddie found his first novel, *Blue River* — a trade-sized paperback that someone had sent to Wallis. Mickey wanted to read it right away. He told his roommate author that he would discuss it with him when he finished it.

Eddie Dense was the lead character in *Blue River*. The story began when young Eddie's dysfunctional parents separated in

Council Bluffs, and his mother moved him and his older sister, Sara, into a new double-wide mobile home he called FIKSHEN. Eddie's best friend and neighbor was David, an affable African-American kid his age whose younger brother, Charles, tragically drowned in the nearby Missouri River. Eddie and Dave were inseparable brothers until Jenna moved into the neighborhood and Dave fell in love with her. Again, tragedy struck Eddie's world when Dave and Jenna died of carbon monoxide poisoning while parked at night beside the river. Eddie was devastated. It was Dave who had talked about the elusive "blue river" — a metaphor for consciousness and inner peace. So when Eddie graduated from high school, he hit the road in his van and wrote *Blue River,* believing he would reach his "blue river" while selling his self-published book.

Mickey read *Blue River* all that afternoon and evening, and the next day he was ready to discuss what he'd read with Eddie. Mickey wanted to know if the story was true.

"Mostly," Eddie answered. "Of course I took some artistic liberties to make the story more interesting; but for the most part, it is true to the events that happened."

"How did you get from where you were in *Blue River* to where you were driving a cab in Council Bluffs?"

Eddie explained how he had met Lauren in the San Francisco area, and she helped him get his book published. The difficulties selling his book were incredible, and eventually it caused the writer and Lauren to split. Eddie scoured the Southwest, selling his book from business to business and reaching his low point in Oklahoma when he had Lauren fly out to him for a "lost weekend." It was soon after that reunion that Eddie's van, with Eddie inside of it, was tossed off a ferry in a storm while crossing a giant lake. At the bottom of the lake, Eddie managed to escape from the van and float to the lake's surface on a foam mattress. Then he floated unconscious on the surface in the throes of a vivid dream.

Eddie dreamed he was in a coma for several years. During that time his sister Sara marketed his book for him, making it an international bestseller. When he came out of his long coma, he learned he had a son. Les Dense was a troubled teen who also

169

ended up tragically drowning after getting close to Eddie. Then Eddie woke up from his dream on the shore of that lake, truly conscious and having reached his own "blue river." He returned home in a new state of consciousness.

After working for a few years in his parents' bar, he was finding it difficult to sustain his new state of consciousness being constantly surrounded by people caught in addiction and hopelessness. He decided he could better serve these people by transporting them than feeding their addictions, so he bought a cab and went to work.

"So then how did you end up here?" Mickey asked.

"Your father sent me a letter. He had been sent a copy of *Blue River* by one of his readers, and he found many similarities in our writing and marketing styles. He wanted me to help him write and market his last novel to his readers. I agreed to the proposal, but my father died and then my mother had health issues that prevented me from coming here to Prairieville when I had originally planned. Once I was able to help my mother get her health problems under control and her business affairs in order, I was able to fulfill my obligation to your father. By that time, he had already written and marketed several more novels, plus he had drafted *Superland.*

"I think what primarily drew your father and me together was the fact that we were both searching for that higher level of consciousness and inner peace ... our own 'blue river.' And we did that primarily by living our lives through the books we wrote."

"Sweet. Can you help me get there?" Mickey asked.

"Maybe. It's up to you."

"I'm willing. I meditate every day."

"That's good."

"How do I start?"

"Pay attention to your thoughts and go with your feelings."

"And increase the gaps in my mind."

"That's right," Eddie affirmed.

"Was my father there?"

"Oh, yes. He'd seen the light when he landed Superland here."

"For me it's about reaching a higher frequency in my music."

"Yes ... That's what paying attention to your feelings can do. The greatest gift your father gave you, Mickey, is the freedom to play your music. You don't have to worry about making a living first and then finding the time and energy to play."

"Yeah. Why did you stop writing after you returned home?"

"I didn't believe I had anything important to say. So if your music is important to you ... play it, Mickey. Play it for as long as you can."

"I will."

Sophomore Katie Spink read *Superland* twice when Mickey gave it to her. Nothing that was revealed in it about her mother's life surprised her. She knew her mother had been cheating on her father years before her chicanery with Lloyd Apple. One thing that came through clearly in the book was that the love the author had for Mickey was akin to the love her father had for her.

Because of her counseling, she was able to process her relationship with her mother. And she knew that Johnny was making the same positive progress regarding his father.

Not having her brother or Johnny around in school made her spend more time with her father. Karl had no interest in reading *Superland,* though, or finding out more dirt on his dead ex-wife. "I'm moving on with my life," Karl smiled to Katie. "And I'm delighted you're in therapy. To see you happy makes me happy," he told his daughter.

October brought an explosion of colors to Kenwick. It was Katie's favorite time of the year. And for the first time in her life, Katie was paying attention to boys. One boy in particular was Johnny Apple. She would go to his house and find him on a high after working that day. She would listen to his endless details about his flight in weather that changed minute by minute at the various altitudes. She asked him if she could fly with him.

"I'm not insured yet for passengers," he answered her, "but as soon as I am, then you can."

After each visit with him, she would be on a high thinking about what it would be like flying with him and soaring so close to heaven. Usually she would return home to make supper for her father, preparing healthy meals she had learned from a cookbook her mother never used. After her father changed out of his gray elevator work clothes, she would talk about Johnny. He could tell she had a girl's crush on the young pilot, and he dismissed it as temporary.

On the first Saturday in October, wearing a gold-colored wool scarf around her neck, she walked across Prairieville carrying *Superland* back to Mickey. How strange it was to her that Mr. P was gone and now her brother owned this incredible land that she loved as much as Mr. P had. A pair of yellow warblers fluttered out from the golden grasses a few feet in front of her, startling her to a giggle. She watched them fly off and noticed the last flowers of fall that were now shriveled brown atop leaning stems from the recent first frost.

Yes, this was Katie's favorite time of year. She could dress in warm colors that diminished her freckles and made her body feel like dancing for the pure joy of life. When she was about a hundred yards from the barn, she heard the sound of a small plane in flight overhead, and she stopped to watch it's westward trek. Images of her riding with Johnny into the same blue ether of sky made her heart swell with love and anticipation of living their dreams together.

Then came the mysterious sounds of LAT 44 from the open barn, and she stopped again to listen. Again she marveled at the changes he'd made, causing her to lose her busy mind in a maelstrom of musical runs and chords she had never heard him play before.

Parked outside the barn was a vehicle she didn't recognize. She entered the barn and saw Hanna, remembering her from the Fourth of July barbeque. Hanna was standing close to Mickey, and it was obvious that Hanna liked her brother more than Johnny. Katie waved to them, not wanting to impose.

"Hey!" Mickey smiled.

"Hi!" Hanna smiled.

"We were just headed for the DQ. Wanna come?" her brother asked.

"Oh, no. I just stopped by to return this," she said as she handed him the manuscript.

"Eddie's home if you want to hang out. You can give it to him," Mickey said.

Eddie was glad to see Katie. She was curious if Mickey was dating Hanna and asked Eddie.

"I don't know," Eddie answered. "She came home from college for the weekend and stopped by to see him."

"Does he like her?"

"I don't know."

"I was just curious. Johnny used to like her."

"I know. They're just friends now." As she handed him the manuscript he said, "Oh, what did you think of *Superland?*"

"It was good."

"Anything in there upset you?"

"No, not really. Nothing really surprised me ... except for Lloyd's spying and fooling around. Mr. P was always good to Lloyd. He sure didn't deserve to be treated like that."

A knock on the front door interrupted their conversation. It was Johnny. He had sold Superland to Wade for thirty grand, so he and Wade were going to dismantle its wings and load it onto a transporter equipped with a cable hoist that was hitched to Wade's truck parked near the barn. When Eddie asked him if they needed any help, Johnny said he might need help positioning the plane on the transporter.

While Johnny and Wade worked on removing the wings, Mickey returned in Hanna's red Volvo and both went inside the barn. Johnny was surprised to see Hanna. Jealousy was still there, for Hanna looked beautiful and had obviously chosen his friend over him.

"I'll pick you up at 6:30," Hanna told Mickey, then left in her car.

"You two dating?" Johnny asked above Wade's power drill removing another bolt from the remaining wing.

"No ... or I don't know. We're going to Dakota Falls tonight for dinner at a place she likes."

Johnny nodded and was awkwardly quiet after that.

Katie watched the men load the wings after positioning Superland on the rear end of the transporter. Katie could see that Johnny wanted to get the job done and leave as soon as possible.

When Johnny and Wade drove away with Superland, Mickey stared at the empty space where his father's plane had been stored. He absently told Katie, "Johnny isn't happy about me going out with Hanna."

"I could tell he was upset," Katie agreed. "She's not Johnny's type, anyway."

"And am I?" Mickey returned.

"Johnny's too short for her. You're tall," she said.

"That's no reason. She flies and so does he."

"Just see how you hit it off tonight. It's your first date, right?"

"Yeah ... first date ever," Mickey quipped.

Mickey wore his black cotton dress shirt with gray corduroy pants and his black slip-on dress shoes — the same outfit he'd worn to his father's memorial service. Eddie loaned him fifty bucks since Mickey only had twenty bucks cash left from the money Hanna had paid him for playing at her party.

"Hanna said she's buyin' our dinner, so I prob'ly won't spend much money," Mickey said.

"You should have cash on ya just the same," Eddie advised.

"If I spend any of your fifty, I'll go to the bank ATM tomorrow and give it back to ya."

"No problem ... just have a good time."

From the desk window, Mickey could see headlights coming down the lane at 6:30 sharp. "She's here. Don't wait up," he joked to his grinning roommate.

Hanna was dressed like a rich college girl, the same way her sorority sisters dressed. She wore expensive designer jeans with a navy blue vest over a revealing white blouse. Her clothes were accented with expensive jewelry on her neck, wrists, and most of her fingers. She smelled of sweet perfume, and her hair was up, making her look five years older and stunningly beautiful to the eye. She wore no lipstick, only a hint of rouge. She maintained most of her summer tan with the help of a tanning bed in Mankato.

Leaving Prairieville, she removed a full half-pint bottle of cherry-flavored vodka she'd bought from an older sorority sister. She offered it to her date after taking a sip herself.

"No thanks."

"C'mon ... just a sip," she giggled.

Mickey took a sip and it burned his throat.

"What do you think?" Hanna giggled again.

"It's diff'rent." Mickey cleared his throat, causing her to laugh hard as they headed out of Kenwick toward I-90.

On the drive to the City she sipped her vodka now and then and talked about her life in Mankato. She rambled on about cute guys, easy classes, and the many friends she'd made in her sorority house. "It's so good to get away from my parents. It's ... like I'm totally free for the first time."

"I know what you mean," Mickey agreed, referring to his escape from the farm.

"I told all my friends about you and how you played your music at my party. They all want you to come play at our sorority house."

"Uh ... I don't think so."

"Why not?" she whined as he declined another sip.

Hanna and Mickey went to the same upscale restaurant his father had taken his mother to when they were dating. It was the same place his mother had taken him to with the Cadman on his seventeenth birthday. Mickey and Hanna both had a fabulous prime rib dinner and enjoyed a blues rendition of "Stormy." Hanna scooted close to her date and kissed him on the lips. Mickey stayed away from alcohol, yet his date was able to buy mixed drinks with a fake ID she got in Mankato. She was all over Mickey, and he was not liking it.

On the short walk to her car after leaving the restaurant, "Stormy" suggested they get a room at the Best Western downtown with her credit card. Mickey politely declined and drove them back to Prairieville. Rejected Hanna was able to drive herself home after kissing her date goodnight without hard feelings.

The next morning had turned cold from a blast of Canadian air that blew at thirty miles an hour all morning. Eddie had a roaring fire going when Mickey came downstairs wearing a pair of his father's gold-colored flannel pajamas.

"How was your date?" Eddie asked.

"Okay," Mickey yawned and stretched.

"You have a good time?"

"Yeah ... I guess," he yawned again, not wanting to talk about Hanna.

At the breakfast table in the kitchen, Eddie told Mickey that he had called his ex-girlfriend, Lauren, in San Diego while he was on his date.

"Yeah? Way to go, Eddie! What happened? Is she married?"

"No. And I was amazed when she told me she was single. We talked for an hour. She's open to flying here for a visit."

"Sweet!"

"I couldn't believe her number was listed and she answered the phone in that same voice I always loved."

"What's she been doin'?"

"She's a licensed massage therapist in Pacific Beach. She has a little office a block from her apartment. She's doing great."

"She'll have to give you a massage," Mickey smiled.

"Yeah. She said she would."

"Sweet. What made you call her?"

"Your date with Hanna. I got to thinkin' about her ... and just called her. Do you think you'll keep seeing Hanna?"

"Yeah ... as friends. She likes to date guys at school now."

"That's cool. At least she's up front about it."

"Yeah," Mickey agreed.

Later that afternoon Hanna called Mickey to tell him she had a good time on their date and looked forward to seeing him again in a few weeks.

Lauren's Visit

Eddie's eyes were relaxed as he watched the passengers off-loading their flight at the Dakota Falls Regional Airport. He saw her coming into view — her almond skin flawless and her brown, frizzy hair styled the way he always remembered it, wild and fanned out. Pulling her carry-on bag, he could see that she was as laid back as ever in her faded jeans, wool purple sweater, and worn hiking boots. Her smiling green eyes came up to meet him with a light that saw him clearly.

"Hi, Eddie," she said with warmth and fondness.

"Hi. You look good, Lauren."

"So do you."

They embraced like old lovers, holding each other for several moments after too many years of separation. The smell of jasmine on her brought back vivid memories of their past life together.

At the luggage belt she retrieved her cased, portable massage table.

"Sweet," Eddie smiled.

On the drive to Prairieville, Lauren was elated to be in a part of the country she had never seen before. She was impressed by the wide, open spaces and the markedly slower pace of life in rural America. They caught up on the years since they'd parted. She was really surprised he was only working on his second book.

"I thought you'd have published several books by now. Only because you were *so ambitious,* Eddie." After you called I reread your revised second printing of *Blue River* ... and all over again I was elated for you that you had reached your elusive 'blue river.' Then you drove a cab. I laughed out loud when I imagined you driving a cab. That was a real shocker, Eddie Dense," Lauren laughed.

By the time they took the LeRoy exit, Eddie had explained how he came to Prairieville, how he was drawn there by Mr. P's letter, and he gave her an overview of the events that had happened since arriving there a little over a year ago.

Upon listening to Eddie talk about the people involved in Wallis Pond's life Lauren said, "Eddie, you have a book here!"

"Yes. It was Mr. P who inspired me to write again. And I doubt that I would've called you if I hadn't come here. We don't have a son, do we?"

"No," she laughed. "I've been living my life knowing I create my reality. Everyone I meet and every place I see is here because I created it in my reality. Ever since I began seeing the world in this way, I've prospered and made my life a more interesting journey. I wanted you to see that. It was important to me. I admired you for writing and living your life willfully until you reached your goal. Is your next book being written in the same, intentional way you wrote your first book?"

"No ... it's different. I want my characters to surprise me ... and I'm staying out of their way."

"That is different," she agreed.

He slowed his car upon turning onto the lane at the entrance to Prairieville. The view from the winding lane with its wind-swept gullies and the looming quartzite cliff line captivated his guest. Then she saw the barn and the house in the distance.

"Oh, Eddie ... this is nice. Real nice."

After parking in front of the house she heard Mickey's guitar playing LAT 44. "Mickey?" she queried.

Eddie nodded yes.

She stood outside his car listening to Mickey's song, impressed by its haunting melody.

"He plays one song ... and it's all his," Eddie said.

When carrying her massage table up the wheelchair ramp, Eddie turned back to Lauren. She had stopped wheeling her suitcase to stare at the cliff line, mesmerized by its raw beauty. "This is incredible, Eddie. No wonder you live here."

Eddie got a fire going and poured each of them a glass of red wine.

She walked around the living room sensing this had been the home of an old writer. "I love that desk," she said.

"He wrote most of his books there."

"And the view is incredible. I can see you living here, Eddie."

"For now," he smiled.

"How long will you live here?"

"I don't know. Until I leave."

"I could spend my whole life here ... But don't get scared. That's not a proposal," she laughed.

Mickey came into the house and met Lauren. He couldn't help but be impressed with her easy manner and natural beauty.

"I love your music," she said. "And you taught yourself to play by ear. Amazing!"

Mickey had read a little bit about Lauren in *Blue River,* and had thought about her that night on his date with Hanna. Lauren had been Eddie's first girlfriend, and Mickey feared having intimacy with Hanna for what might happen to change his whole life.

Mickey liked being around Eddie and Lauren. They were "together" like no other couple he had ever seen. Lauren sat close to Eddie on Mr. P's old leather sofa, and Mickey could see that their eyes had light emanating from them — the same fine shards of light that he'd seen on his mother's diamonds that the Cadman had given her. He sat across from the relaxed couple in his father's high-back, brown leather chair and listened intently to everything they had to say. Eddie mentioned that in the therapy sessions, he'd seen that he was denying himself a close relationship with a woman because of his dysfunctional parents' constant arguing at home and at the bar.

"What else have you learned about yourself?" Lauren asked.

"That I am not my parents," Eddie said.

"I'm in therapy too," Mickey said to Lauren.

"Oh, really? And what have you learned?"

"That I have a bunch of anger toward my mother and my grandparents who raised me on this boring farm. They withheld love and material provision from me, so I withheld love and help with the farming chores from them."

"Have you heard of neuro-emotional bodywork?" Lauren asked Mickey.

He shook his head no.

"I've been trained and licensed to release emotions stored in the body ... toxic things we hold on to. It's specialized bodywork."

"Really? You didn't tell me that. Nobody does that kind of bodywork around here," Eddie stated.

"Can you do that kind of bodywork on me?" Mickey asked.

"Sure. Tomorrow afternoon. But you have to fast for at least twelve hours beforehand."

"Okay. I will."

"She brought her table," Eddie told Mickey as he pointed to the encased massage table.

"Sweet."

Eddie made dinner for them — a large salad with tofu that Mickey didn't care for. Lauren had been a vegetarian since before she had met Eddie, and she loved the meal he made for her.

At dawn Eddie took Lauren for a walk around Prairieville. She wore one of Eddie's winter coats in the near-freezing temps, and she truly loved everything on the land that her keen eyes saw. From the pond she saw the long line of mystery rocks and headed there with Eddie hand in hand.

"Mr. P said it was built by Native Americans to mark the sun's planting and harvest time line."

"This is so cool, Eddie!" she sang with joy as she sat on the cold stone wall in a state of pure reverential awe. Lauren had the ability to see every living thing, even noticing the frequent wind changes that Prairieville was known for. A family of woodpeckers hammering into the blue spruce thrilled her. She watched and listened to them with such rapt attention that Eddie too became more joyful.

In the early afternoon Lauren set up her massage table near the burning fireplace, preparing for Mickey's bodywork. She worked on Eddie's neck and upper back for twenty minutes until

Mickey came downstairs. Eddie went upstairs to give them privacy; he knew from experience that this kind of bodywork could be intense, at the very least.

On his back, clad only in boxers, Mickey's body was holding onto emotional pain in his solis area below his rib cage and in his chest area. Working deeper and deeper with her strong fingers, she told him to see and let go of anything that came up for him; and to shout, cry, or scream from the pain her trained hands were reaching as she kneaded and dug her fingers into his tender muscles.

"OUCH! OW!" Mickey exclaimed repeatedly from the pain he felt.

She told him to think about his mother and his grandparents who had angered him over the years. It was when lying on his belly and Lauren was probing for more emotional trauma in his lower back that Mickey became nauseous. Gurgling negative past emotions became active, and he'd spit them out of his mouth into the wastebasket positioned within arm's reach for such releases. Near the end of his first hour-long session, he began sobbing uncontrollably with streams of toxic tears plopping into the receptacle.

Exhausted and face down, Mickey was covered with a sheet by Lauren. She told him to breathe and let go of anything that came up for him. Then Lauren went upstairs, washed her hands, and informed Eddie, "Mickey had a really good session." Eddie wanted to pay her for Mickey's bodywork, but Lauren refused. She told him it was her gift to them, and any bodywork she did at Prairieville was "on the house."

"I'd like a session too," Eddie smiled.

"You're next," she pointed.

Later that day Mickey was still exhausted form his session with Lauren when Hanna called him from Mankato, telling him she was coming home for the weekend and wanted to see him. Mickey was receptive, looking forward to seeing her. *Did my bodywork change my feelings for Hanna?* he wondered.

Eddie's session was easier for Lauren, and she discovered he was in pretty good emotional shape.

That evening Eddie took Lauren out to dinner in Dakota Falls to an East Indian restaurant she really enjoyed. After dinner they walked along the river on the River Walk, stopping to watch a large flock of great Canadian geese that adopted the Big Sioux River as home most of the year.

Eddie was also feeling better after his session, and he told Lauren that he and Mickey had both decided they didn't need any more counseling with their psychologist.

"Why did you go to counseling?" Lauren asked.

"So Mickey would. And Mr. P thought it was a good idea after Mickey lost his mother. I was stuck, Lauren. Until you came, I might've kept myself isolated ... not even concerned about meeting a woman. Look ... I know it's fast, but I'd like you to move here ... see how you like it here with me."

"Eddie, I've got my clients ... an office ... and my apartment. I can't just leave it all. Why don't you move out to San Diego and live with me? You can come back if it doesn't work out."

"I can't. Mr. P gave me two hundred thousand dollars to market his last book. And when he decided not to publish it, he let me keep the money. I know he wanted me to stay at Prairieville until Mickey is older. We made an informal agreement that I can't break. Besides that, I *want* to stay here. I'm here to help Mickey in some inexplicable way ... like having you come here. I know you've helped me already."

"Eddie, I do love you. I think you know that. I'm helping so many people with my work. I think we have to stay where we are. I could fly out often ... until you got tired of me."

"I'm selfish. I want you with me all the time ... from now on."

She kissed him and they held each other beside the river. Eddie understood her situation and didn't press her. "Perhaps a visit each way once a month would be good," he said.

She agreed and kissed him again.

The next day Eddie took Lauren to Palisades State Park, the place Wallis Pond would go to rest, write, and fish close to the one-room cabin beside the water. Since Lauren loved the ocean,

Palisades was the closest body of water to Prairieville that Eddie knew.

"This is beautiful, Eddie," she remarked. "It reminds me of one of those hidden gems of nature in northern California that just suddenly appears and surprises you ... giving you this lasting feeling all day that you've been someplace special."

They meditated together, back to back, on the water's edge, breathing in the cold October air that was crystal clean and invigorating.

Earlier that morning, they awoke to a healthy breakfast prepared by Mickey. Their young host had announced he'd had the best sleep he'd ever had and was grateful to Lauren, giving her work all the credit. Extra flattery came her way when Mickey added, "Too bad you don't live here, Lauren. You could keep us healthy with your bodywork."

It was Katie who saw how Mickey was different somehow, yet she couldn't tell what it was about him that had changed. She told her father, "He seems more loose ... not as stiff."

On her last night at Prairieville in Eddie's room, Lauren told Eddie, "I can see you created Prairieville from a space of no resistance. You were able to come here after completing your business with your family. You didn't run away to this. This is where you should be, Eddie."

"And you?" he asked.

"It's been a wonderful visit here with you. And I admit that I'm torn and confused about being here with you and going back to my home. But like you ... I will know when it's right for me. But I do want to see you again, Eddie. Soon."

"Lauren, you are so smart and know what's best for you now. I have no problem or resistance to what you want. I do love you and know I will be a better man with you in my life. I don't get many chances to be with someone like you."

At the airport he watched her smiling face rise and fade away from his view on the escalator. Then she was gone. Another moment of separation came over him and passed through him. Like Wallis Pond, he too had seen the ego's false love come and go, then embraced his aloneness by feeling all of its intensity. Lauren's healing touch would stay with him for as long as he lived. This time — unlike in Oklahoma — there was no pathetic ego longing for her return. Only the memory of the real love he felt from her healing touch that he knew was also needed in San Diego.

Change of Heart

Around mid-November after the first snowfall, Johnny was hired by a corporation in Dakota Falls to begin training for his commercial pilot's license. He had begun his training with Wade Hampton flying private jets. In less than two years, at the age of twenty-one, he'd be flying professionally and making eighty thousand a year. Johnny wanted to get his own apartment in Marshall. His mother approved his decision, since she was living alone well and was sustained by her thriving ironing business. Soon Johnny found a furnished apartment a few miles from the airfield and moved in before anyone other than his mother knew he was living on his own.

When Katie dropped by the Apple house, she was surprised to hear from Maxine that Johnny had his own apartment. Katie knew his cell phone number but didn't call him. She was happy for him and wanted to give him his space. Katie left the Apple house and walked to Prairieville and shared the news about Johnny with Mickey and Eddie.

Lauren was flying out to visit Eddie again over the Thanksgiving holiday, and Mickey was looking forward to seeing Hanna again when she came home. Katie's turkey day would be with her father, who was delighted to get half of his retirement money from Marilyn's attorney.

The day of Lauren's arrival, Eddie had finished the first draft of his second novel and was in a celebratory mood. Since he was able to live comfortably on the interest of his savings, he was wanting more and more to have Lauren live with him at Prairieville and begin a new life together.

Lauren didn't bring her massage table this trip. She had been busier than usual in order to schedule this much-needed respite from work. She brought winter clothes with her — and was glad she had when she landed at the frigid airport.

They went straight to a restaurant and shared a bottle of wine over dinner to celebrate their reunion. During dinner Lauren surprised Eddie. "I really got in touch with how I feel about you and how I feel about living here with you. I could let go of everything I have ... because it's temporary ... just like we are. I lost you once for a long time, and it just seems incredible that either of us is available to even be together. I've had a change of heart ... I want to live with you, Eddie Dense."

"You're saying you'll move out of your place and leave your clientele?"

She smiled while nodding yes. "I can pay rent to Mickey, buy my food, and split expenses like we did when we were living together."

"I can cover all that. And that would help you make up the money you'll lose by moving away from your clients. And I can fly out to move you back here. When can you move?"

"I was thinking the end of December ... after giving a month's notice at my apartment and office."

They toasted to their new life together.

On their drive to Prairieville, Lauren talked about how "serendipitous" it was for Eddie to live with Mickey. "It's really so much like that dream you told me about that you had on that lake in Oklahoma. You are the right age to be Mickey's father, and I can see a closeness in your relationship that is very much like a father and son."

"Yes ... the dream continues, doesn't it?" Eddie said with a chuckle.

"Yes! It's just incredible how you were meant to be at Prairieville with Mickey after his father died."

"That's why it's important to me that you read my first draft of *Different*."

"*Different* ... that's the title?"

"Uh-huh."

"I want to read it right away," Lauren said enthusiastically.

Lauren read Eddie's first draft for three hours in bed that night, resisting her temptation to edit it and just taking in the story. She went to sleep having read the first half without discussing it. She got up early the next morning and finished the story at Pond's lamp-lit desk downstairs. When Eddie came downstairs after shaving and showering, they sat on the sofa and had a hot cup of Lauren's tea she'd brought with her.

"Well ...?" Eddie asked, referring to what she thought of his book.

"It's good, Eddie. I was impressed. The characters were well developed and held my interest ... and there were surprises. It is different from *Blue River* — not nearly as intense and traumatic — and I like that fact that it takes place here. You really captured Prairieville. But what I really like about the story is that it's all about transformation in a mad world of unconsciousness."

"That about covers it," Eddie agreed. He got up from the sofa with his first draft in hand, walked over to the fireplace, and began putting page after page into the fire until his entire manuscript was ashes.

"What are you doing?" Lauren asked after the first couple of pages met the flames.

"I'm destroying my book."

"Why?"

"Because ... it's worthless."

"Worthless? Are you crazy?"

"Not anymore. It's a piece of worthless tripe. I realized after Mr. P died that I didn't have it in me to write a good book ... a *really* good book. I don't want to write anymore, Lauren. I have you now. I want to live my life any way but as a writer from now on. It's a lonely life that I saw up close when Mr. P was alive. I don't want that life for me ... for us."

"Are you sure?"

"I couldn't destroy it if it had any value."

"But all the time you spent writing it ..."

"It's fiction, Lauren. It's not important. There are real lives to live for here. I want to put all my energy into living a real life. No more fiction."

She went over to him and hugged him. That's when Eddie told her he had lost her because his first book was more important to him than she was.

"Mr. P was able to give up his last book because of the people who were in his life here. I was able to give up my book because I want to have a life with you ... now. There's an art to living well, and writing is living within yourself. I don't want to live that way ever again. That's *my* change of heart. I want us to live every moment of our lives in the present. Our job is to teach each other to do that. I would miss thousands of hours of being here if I kept working on something as selfish as a story that means nothing to anybody. I want us to go upstairs and hold each other until I fall asleep. And when I wake up ... I will be new again ... ready to live my life in a brand new way that I know Mr. P wanted for himself and for me. He gave me this gift by paying me to stay here. I see now what he wanted me to see ... but could never tell me. He was lost in his work and too old to change his life. So he changed me. Just like for Mickey, he wanted me to be 'different' and live a real life."

They went upstairs and fell asleep holding each other — each knowing that when they awoke, their lives would be different.

Lauren and Eddie were committed to living each moment as if it was created by them — a nature-perfect order of things that was validated consciously from the moment they awakened from their nap.

Mickey saw firsthand this new way of living when Hanna came to Prairieville to visit him later that evening. Mickey introduced his friend to Lauren.

"Lauren, this is Hanna."

"Pleased to meet you, Hanna."

Hanna and Mickey were struck by the attentiveness Eddie and Lauren displayed.

"So Mickey tells me you live in San Diego."

"Yes, but I'm moving here soon."

"Really?" Mickey said with surprise.

"Yes. Eddie and I will be staying here for as long as Mickey wants us to."

"Sweet! You can stay here for as long as you want!"

"How's school?" Eddie asked Hanna.

"Oh ... okay. I like the friends I've made. I haven't declared a major yet ... but I know I want to teach. Something ... but I'm not sure what," Hanna confessed with genuine sweetness.

"The perfect way of serendipity will take you along your perfect path," Lauren said.

"My dad believes in serendipity! He talks about these little miracles that happen every day in his life," Hanna laughed.

"Have you met Hanna's dad?" Eddie asked Mickey.

Mickey looked sheepishly at his girlfriend until they burst into laughter. Hanna answered for Mickey, "Tonight we're having dinner with my parents, and Mickey is meeting them for the first time."

"That should be fun," Lauren smiled at Mickey's apprehension.

Lauren and Eddie walked outside in the cold November air to watch the young couple drive away in Hanna's car. "She's sweet," Lauren said.

"Yes ... and beautiful," Eddie added.

Eddie noticed a light was on in the west window of the barn. They walked inside the barn over to the workbench where Mickey played his guitar. The absence of Superland was obvious in the vacant space the plane once occupied. Before turning off the light, Eddie saw a green one-hit pipe cylinder inside an ashtray that held the burnt remains of marijuana. Eddie dismissed it as an artist's experimentation with altered states of thought patterns, and Lauren agreed. They left the cold barn after Eddie turned off the light.

The sat close to each other on the couch in front of the burning fireplace when Lauren realized she'd never seen a television set in the house.

"Mickey doesn't want one and neither do I. His father never watched TV. Mr. P said it was food for a fearful mind."

"I gave it up too. You have to be careful what you pay attention to. And I got so much more done when I stopped watching it."

"I was thinking ... what if we made it our goal to help Mickey put his music out there?"

"And he only plays one song."

"That's right."

"So we help him put his song out there?" Lauren said with a hint of surprise in her voice.

"We can't see what his music can do for us. We can only see what we can do for him. He's given us a place to live. His father has given me more money than I could save in twenty or thirty years. And since he lives here, we'll be able to see that we are helping him live a life that reflects our own lives. And I know the world is a bottomless pit of people and causes in need ... and we can't help them all. But Mickey's real and his music is good. And he plays right here day and night in that barn. Now he's smokin' weed and has no goals for his music ... at least that I know of. You can give him bodywork and I can put his music on a CD."

"I don't know if a nineteen-year-old kid wants to be pushed in any direction by us or anybody," Lauren said.

"I think you should hear all of his song and we should talk after that. And if you don't feel he has real talent ... we won't get involved."

"We could sit here forever listening to Mickey's music, living our lives in this paradise away from the frenetic world ... and maybe that would be fine. My father left me some money, and we don't have to work if we don't want to. But we have to do something for our spiritual growth. I'll listen to his song and we'll see."

Dinner with Hanna's parents went well at the Storm house, and they stayed up late watching movies. When driving Mickey home she told him that she'd been "seeing" a guy — a senior at school named Jeff.

"Does 'seeing' mean you're sleeping with him?" Mickey asked.

"Yeah ... a few times," Hanna smiled.

"You must like him."

Yeah ... and I like you too. I wanted to be honest and tell you."

"I appreciate that. Does he wear protection?"

She giggled after a long pause, then explained that they were both careful.

"I'll bet you're mad at me," she pouted and looked back and forth between Mickey and the windshield.

"No, I'm not mad. We can still be friends."

"I shouldn't have told you. How come guys can be with lots of girls, but when a girl wants to play the field she's a tramp ... or just a friend?"

"Remember serendipity, Hanna. You have to live your life for you ... not for me. You might really like this Jeff or meet someone else you like even more. But what you're doing is dangerous. That's how I was born."

"That's serendipity!" she laughed.

"That's a good way to look at it. I was a fortunate accident," he laughed with her.

When Hanna dropped off Mickey, he kissed her goodnight and told her to be careful.

Lauren and Eddie were still up when Mickey returned home. They listened to him explain why he couldn't date Hanna. They agreed with his mature explanation.

"I'm impressed, Mickey," Lauren told him.

* * * * *

Lauren and Eddie stood close to the space heater glowing in the barn while Mickey played LAT 44 for twenty-seven minutes on Thanksgiving Day. Afterwards, Lauren hugged the musician and told him how much she was impressed with his music. "Real love," she called it.

It was during their vegetarian dinner prepared by Lauren that they discussed marketing LAT 44.

"I know you don't need to sell your music for the money," Eddie said, "but do you have any desire to put your LAT 44 out there in the world?"

"I thought about using my father's list and selling a CD to his loyal readers. But then I remembered how he wanted me to do something different from anything he'd done in his life. I couldn't come up with anything except how I've always wanted to reach a higher frequency with my music and play something that nobody has heard before. I don't know if I can do that."

"You have done that," Lauren told him. "You've created real love. You're there, Mickey."

"Yes, I agree," Eddie said. "But marketing a song by an independent artist would only get lost in retail outlets. Here and there people would buy it."

They ate in silence, waiting for something to come to them. Then Mickey said, "What if the world doesn't care? Can't I play my music here ... and have that be enough?"

Eddie and Lauren looked at each other, then Eddie said, "You can do that. It's your life."

"Sweet. I'll play my music for me. That's what I want."

After dinner Mickey walked over to the Spink house to visit Katie and Karl, then he was hoping to catch Johnny at his mother's house for Thanksgiving. As he cut through his land he felt like a big load had been lifted from his shoulders. Passing the pond and heading into the wooded area that ran along Kenwick Road, he felt good that he could just play his music for fun and not be concerned about marketing it to a world that he knew would only dismiss it as "another song." Eddie had told him before leaving his house, "If anything, your father has given you the freedom to be yourself."

Now he hoped Lauren and Eddie would still live at Prairieville, because he knew he could learn so much from a couple who truly loved and respected each other. He had never seen that before. Ned and Bert had been poor examples for learning how to live well. And no way was he wanting or ready to live alone at Prairieville.

Before heading onto Kenwick Road, he stopped and looked back in the direction of his barn and his house. He could see smoke rising from the fireplace into the gray skies over Prairieville. He thanked his father for bringing Eddie to him and giving him this wonderful place to call his home.

Crossing the road he could see the Christmas lights Katie and Karl had put up recently that lined their modest front-room window.

The Spinks had finished their Thanksgiving dinner and welcomed Mickey inside with a slice of pumpkin pie covered with whipped cream that Katie had made. Mickey talked about Lauren moving into the house after Christmas and what a great couple they were to be around.

Mickey was surprised to hear that Johnny had his own place in Marshall. He and Katie went to Maxine's house to get his address, and they saw Johnny's truck was parked in his mother's driveway.

Johnny was elated to see his friends and drove them over to his apartment to show it to them. During the drive he told them about his new job with Mercury Industries and how he'd soon be licensed to fly their corporate jet after only a few hundred more hours of flight training.

"It's all coming together for you, Johnny. You're living your dream to fly," Katie said.

They sat around Johnny's sparsely furnished one-bedroom apartment looking at photos of jets in the training manuals he was studying. Later, Johnny drove them to the airfield hangar and showed them the interior of the corporate jet he'd be flying. The young pilot stated proudly that his million-dollar aircraft's plush passenger seats were top of the line. They were so comfortable and spacious that passengers often fell asleep on quick flights to Dakota Falls.

"How come it's here at the Marshall Airfield?" Mickey asked.

"The CEO lives here. Mr. Pollack owns the company. Wade, my instructor, introduced me to him and recommended me when he heard Mr. Pollack was looking for a local pilot. He pays me three hundred a week and pays for Wade to train me."

"Sweet."

Mickey asked Johnny if he wanted to come over to Prairieville to see Eddie again and to meet Lauren. Katie rode along to Prairieville because she wanted to see Eddie and Lauren together.

"You're the boy who can fly!" Lauren exclaimed to Johnny. "I've heard so much about you. I wish I could've seen you fly your planes from the cliff line. Eddie told me how impressed Mr. P was with your flying skills."

Sitting around the cozy front room with a fire going, both Katie and Johnny stated they too were finished with therapy and had gotten enough out of it to move on with their lives. Lauren could see that Katie was "smitten" with Johnny, observing how she looked at him with an obvious girl's crush on the boy who could fly.

When Katie went into the kitchen to watch Lauren prepare some hot ginger tea, Lauren complimented Katie on her sense of style, noting the burgundy wool sweater with its silver-threaded patterns shaped into angels.

"Thanks ... I made it myself."

"You're really good, Katie. How long have you been making your clothes?"

"A long time. I'd like to design clothes when I graduate from high school. But I don't want to be one of those fashion designers who make clothes for those skinny, scowling models. No way. I want to make organic, earthy clothes for real people living on modest incomes ... like me," she stated with such animated perkiness that Lauren had to ask if she'd make her a sweater for the coming winter.

"Sure."

"Oh, I'll pay you for it. I want to. Do you need to measure me?"

"No, I can see what size you are," Katie stated confidently.

"Should I pick a color?"

"I know what looks good for you."

"Don't tell me. I want to be surprised."

"Okay," Katie laughed. After a moment she said, "You seem to be perfect for Eddie. You're both ... so real."

"Thank you, Katie. What a nice thing to say."

"Don't tell Johnny, but I'm making him an aviator scarf for Christmas."

"That's cool. Isn't it incredible how young he is, and soon he'll be flying jets for a big company?"

"Yes, but he's been flying for a long time ... so it doesn't surprise me."

"All three of you are so talented. This must be a creative place to live."

"Mr. P always encouraged us. He gave us the confidence to do our own thing. He's even paying for fashion school if I want to go. I made him a lap blanket for his birthday when I first moved here, and he was so thrilled. I saw tears in his eyes. He's the one who inspired me to keep making clothes for people. I wish you could've met him, Lauren. He was really special. I told my dad how Mr. P is the biggest reason why I want to do something really different with my life. He was the one who told me he wanted me to do something really different with my life ... and I will."

"Aw ... that's so sweet."

Later that night Eddie and Lauren talked about the amazing trio of talent that stayed until ten o'clock talking about their hopes and dreams.

"I have never met such a talented group of young people," Lauren declared. "Here's this cute little sophomore in high school who can design and make her clothes with this incredibly advanced sense of style and color that just amazes me, Eddie. And Johnny Apple ... the boy who can fly, who has had to overcome so much. Here he is ... poised to fly corporate jets around the country. And he's only nineteen!"

"I know ... I know! That's why I wanted to get out of my head writing some unimportant novel ... so I can see these kids live their incredible lives. All of them are awake, Lauren!"

"I know! And they all loved Mr. P. What a gift he gave them ... to be such a positive influence in their lives!"

Yes. That's exactly what I want to do here, Lauren. Otherwise my life is wasted just as much as it would be writing another useless book. Mr. P made me see that. He protected his writing by not claiming Mickey for most of Mickey's life. Boy, did he ever show me how I was headed down that same road ... and he did it without saying a word.

After Lauren flew back home, Eddie felt good about her moving to Prairieville. They agreed that Katie's talent for designing clothes was worth looking into when Lauren returned. And Lauren was now aware how Eddie was needed at Prairieville until Mickey was older and able to live well on his own.

Johnny was detailing the interior of his company's corporate jet when Hanna stopped by the hangar to see him, home for Christmas break. Mickey had told her on the phone about Johnny's new job, and she wanted to congratulate him. Since Mickey had rejected her invitation to go out with her, Hanna was in a "stormy" mood.

Johnny was surprised to see Hanna and even more surprised when she asked him if they could "hang out" while she was home.

A couple days later, Johnny called Hanna and asked her if she wanted to go to a movie in town. Hanna made it obvious in the dark theater that she wanted to see Johnny's apartment.

Hanna was Johnny's first experience with a girl, and she stayed overnight three nights in a row. Johnny never asked her about her social life as Mickey had, although she did tell Johnny that she and Mickey were just friends.

On Christmas Eve when Mickey called Hanna at home to wish her a merry Christmas, she told him that she was dating Johnny and what a "cool guy" he was. Sensing trouble for his friend, Mickey drove over to Johnny's apartment and caught him just as he was leaving with a wrapped gift in hand for Hanna.

"Merry Christmas!" Mickey greeted his surprised friend, who was dressed up like Mickey had never seen before.

"Merry Christmas," Johnny smiled.

Not wanting to spoil Johnny's high, Mickey decided not to tell his friend that Hanna was "dating" a senior at school, and that was the reason he had stopped seeing her. They chatted for a few minutes about Eddie and Lauren, then they made plans to get together for New Year's Eve at Prairieville when Eddie would be in San Diego helping Lauren pack and move.

"Yeah, I'll see ya New Year's Eve, then," Johnny said. "I gotta run."

When Mickey returned home, he talked to Eddie about not being able to warn Johnny about Hanna's other life in Mankato. "I don't want him to get messed up when he's got things goin' so well for himself," Mickey said.

"Next time you see him, ask him if he's serious about Hanna. Then either way you can tell him what you know."

"I don't know ... He was on such a high, Eddie. I wish you would tell him. He'd listen to you. He might think I'm just jealous or somethin'."

Since the beginning of December, Eddie had also been on a high anticipating Lauren's move to Prairieville. And ever since he destroyed his second novel, he had noticed more things around Prairieville that required his attention. That's what he needed — physical projects that left his mind uncluttered compared to a protracted storyline. Like refinishing the hardwood floors that were worn and scuffed in several places on both stories of the house.

Day after day throughout most of December, Eddie sanded the floors with an electric sander. Once they were stripped and sanded, he and Mickey stained and varnished them.

It was Mickey who bought a ten-foot-tall Christmas tree in LeRoy, and put it in the corner of the library near Wallis's desk. He decorated it with three strings of white lights and fallen pine cones found near the Prairieville trees. He had found an old black-and-white photo of Superland and had it framed under glass, then he wrapped it as a gift for Johnny. He placed it against the wall behind the tree.

Eddie and Mickey worked together on a list of projects Mickey could do in and around the house while Eddie was gone helping Lauren move. They worked like a team, always respectful when talking to each other. Mickey — who spent his entire childhood moping around the farm — was now motivated to be helpful and get things done like a mature adult.

For the first time in his life, Mickey felt like he was part of a caring family. When Katie showed up on Christmas Eve with wrapped presents she'd made for Mickey, Eddie and Lauren,

Eddie asked Katie if he and Lauren could open their presents when they returned. He also asked Katie if she would wait to open her present from Eddie and Lauren. Sweet Katie had no problem waiting, and that made Mickey ask Katie if each of them could open presents to each other when Eddie returned with Lauren.

"We'll have a second Christmas together," Katie smiled.

Later that day Katie's Christmas was dashed when she walked to the Apple house to deliver presents to Johnny and Maxine. Hanna and Johnny were kissing in Johnny's parked truck. Johnny was embarrassed for the blushing girl he had known for so many years.

"Is your mom home?" Katie blushed with her arms full of wrapped presents.

"Uh ... yeah," he smiled with his arm still around his new girlfriend.

Katie headed for the front door wishing that she hadn't come by. The scarf she'd made him — with thrilling images of seeing him wear it on the day she finally got to fly with him — seemed trivial now and lost in a green sea of jealousy. Upon delivering her presents to Maxine she made a quick excuse to return home, declining Maxine's invitation to come inside. She ran across the front yard so fast that Johnny didn't have a chance to get Katie's present from inside the house and give it to her.

Long into the night she replayed the kissing scene she'd witnessed. Her brother had told her about Hanna's other lover at school, and she worried that Johnny would be hurt whether he knew it or not. Then she thought Mickey should tell him. Or, better yet, Eddie.

Johnny walked to the Spink house Christmas Day with presents for Katie and Karl from his mother and him. He wore the scarf Katie had made him. They were glad to see him and invited him in for a cup of hot chocolate.

At the Spink kitchen table, Karl and Johnny watched Katie open their present from Maxine and Johnny. It was a new blender that Karl was glad to have since their old blender recently quit running. "Thanks for the scarf," Johnny smiled as

Karl examined his new blender. "How'd you know gray is my favorite color?"

Katie shrugged her shoulders, not wanting to tell him how she knew that he and Mr. P loved gray. "Mickey has a cool present for you. Let's walk over there," Katie suggested.

"Okay. I've got his present too ... but I didn't wrap it," he confessed as he removed a plastic retail sack that held six quality guitar picks.

"Here ... I'll wrap them quick," Katie insisted and took the picks to her room.

"I hear you have a girlfriend," Karl smiled.

"Yeah ... I guess so," Johnny grinned.

On their walk to Prairieville, Johnny showed Katie the expensive watch Hanna gave him for Christmas.

"That's a nice watch," Katie said, resisting the urge to talk about Hanna. But then she had to ask, "What did you get Hanna for Christmas?"

"Sheepskin seat covers for her car. She's always complainin' how cold her car gets."

They walked the rest of the way on Prairieville's cold ground making small-talk about Katie's friends at school and Johnny's jet training.

Eddie and Mickey were in the front room chatting about Johnny and Hanna when the two guests arrived. Eddie made them some of Lauren's hot tea while Johnny opened his framed gift from Mickey.

"Wow! This is nice! Thank you. Where'd you find this?" Johnny asked his friend.

It was in a box in my dad's closet."

Johnny removed the wrapped gift from his pocket and handed it to Mickey. "Merry Christmas."

Mickey was elated with the guitar picks. "Thanks, Johnny. I'll use every one of these."

Now wasn't the time to bring up Hanna's life at Mankato, so Mickey stayed away from asking about her. However, when Eddie asked Johnny what he was doing New Year's Eve Johnny said, "I'll prob'ly do something with Hanna. She does like to party."

Mickey's blinking stare nodded in agreement. He was surprised his friend had abandoned their plans to spend New Year's Eve together without even telling him.

Eddie changed the subject by telling Johnny and Katie that he wanted them to come by for a belated New Year's party after he returned with Lauren.

"What're you going to do in this big house while Eddie's gone?" Johnny asked Mickey.

"I've got some projects around here that'll keep me busy. How about you, Katie? What're you gonna do for New Year's Eve?"

"I'll hang out with my dad. We'll rent some DVDs. Why don't you come over? We can go pick out some movies you'd like."

"I might do that," Mickey said.

On the 29th, the same day Eddie flew to San Diego, Johnny was disappointed that Hanna was going back to Mankato early to celebrate New Year's Eve with her friends. When he asked her if he could drive to Mankato to be with her and celebrate ringing in the new year, Hanna's curt reply floored him. "It's a private party with my sorority sisters and fraternity guys ... sort of an annual tradition."

"Oh," Johnny responded absently with a sinking feeling that told him he wasn't exclusive in Hanna's life.

"Are you mad at me?" she asked with a pout.

"No, no ... you do your thing ... that's cool."

All the way up to December 31st, Johnny fretted about spending New Year's Eve alone. When he was supposed to be studying for his flight exam in three days — a milestone that would advance him to the next level in his training — he found himself not retaining important information and blaming Hanna for failing quiz after quiz in his test manual.

New Year's Eve was Johnny's lowest time of the whole year. He stopped by his mother's house to wish her a happy new year. He told his mother he was going over to Katie's to watch movies with her and Mickey. But when he left his mother's house, he thought about going to the Kenwick Tavern to have one beer.

He stood on the corner of Kenwick and Main unable to go to the place where he'd found his father. Worried about his upcoming exam, he thought it best to go home and study. But then he changed his mind again and walked toward the Spink house.

Karl and Katie were happy to see Johnny at their door and invited him in to watch a movie with them.

"Where's Mickey?" Johnny asked.

Katie told him that Mickey was playing at a party in Mankato. Hanna called him that morning and told him he'd make two hundred bucks if he played.

"Two hundred bucks? He doesn't need the money," Johnny replied with a trace of anger.

Katie knew the real reason her brother was going to play at Hanna's sorority party, but she couldn't tell Johnny the truth. Mickey was going there to see for himself, and for Johnny's sake, if Hanna had changed her ways. Mickey told Katie that he agreed to play at her party after she told him that Johnny wasn't going to be there.

Johnny changed his mind about staying for a movie, telling Katie and Karl he really just stopped by to wish them a happy new year. He had to get back home and study for his big exam in three days.

Again, standing under the streetlight at Kenwick and Main, he checked the expensive gift on his left wrist — a symbol to him that Hanna really liked him. He figured he could be in Mankato before midnight if he left right away.

All the way to Mankato he saw terrible images of Mickey kissing his girl when the clock struck twelve. The fact that Mickey never called him to see if they could ride to the party together — or even to check with him to see if he was going — was a bad sign that something was going on. Johnny Apple wasn't going to be anybody's fool. Especially Mickey Pond's.

On the campus, Johnny found a visitor's parking lot and left his truck there at 11:42 p.m. He asked a student where the sorority houses were located and headed there on foot with his winter hooded jacket covering his head. It was a cold night — only two degrees above zero of bone-chilling, windless cold. Walking across the Mankato campus was like walking through a butcher's freezer in the dark with no signs of life anywhere.

He finally came to a block of brick sorority houses with their esoteric Greek names advertised on the frozen front lawns. He looked for Mickey's Durango and Hanna's Volvo but didn't see them in the lines of parked vehicles on either side of the wide street.

From the sidewalk he could hear the familiar strains of LAT 44 coming from a large, two-story, brick sorority house. Up the steps onto the semi-circular porch, he faltered when he was unable to see inside the front windows. There was no way he was going inside to crash her "private" party and interrupt the "fabulous Mickey Pond's performance." So he paced back and forth with LAT 44 warming him like a festering seed of anger in his belly. His anger grew green tendrils of moving emotions that gurgled and climbed to his throat, sending him to his knees to dry heave at the very edge of the porch covered in darkness. The song was doing this to him — playing haunting chords with gaps of space that plucked long-denied emotions from his belly and saturated his brain with images of his father flying with him from the cliff line. Each second he stayed with each image, Mickey was bringing it closer and closer to a frightening kind of clarity he only experienced when he was flying.

Johnny was struck by the idea that Mickey was playing the loss of his own father, Mr. P. Inside, the audience of some eighty students was all forced to reflect their own losses over the past year. Just then LAT 44 moved to the devastating moment when Johnny found his father in the basement of Kenwick Tavern, causing Johnny to heave traumatic emotions onto the ground below the edge of the porch that he was now holding onto with all his strength. Just like Mr. P, he too was about to crash when all he could see was his father's betrayal to his mother and Mr. P in the long strands of saliva that had come from his belly to his heaving throat. Hurl after hurl released more and more of that awful moment in his life.

Johnny could have run away on weak legs, yet somehow he knew that LAT 44 was purging him of emotions that had to come out. If left dormant, they could destroy him. After what seemed like hours of releasing toxic emotions, the death of his father was gone. With his eyes closed on that cold porch in Mankato, he knew he had been flying with his friend Mickey Pond — riding the winds of LAT 44 with a loyal friend who had returned him safely to the earth with a fresh feeling of right-mindedness and clarity that he hadn't had since he was a boy.

As Johnny wiped his exhausted saliva-soaked hands onto his thighs, he heard the music of a knowing, guiding hand — Eddie Dense — and everything was safe in the present moment in a new world of endless possibilities. He stayed on his knees listening to the beautiful notes that played sounds of hope and joy as each ascending note counted down each second until the new year. To himself he counted down the seconds with Mickey's audience. And when the old year was gone, he opened his eyes and really saw the glow of life all around him. Trees were alive and pulsing in the grip of winter's freeze. The voices of raucous people celebrating a new year were no longer strangers he dared to see. Rather, they were people — young people like himself — who would welcome him and be glad to share this special moment.

His stomach was no longer churning and his body felt light and confident. But then he didn't want to impose his unannounced visit on Hanna or Mickey. It wasn't important to him to see them now.

He headed for his truck, determined to study for his big exam when he got home. None of this petty jealousy stuff or hurt feelings for being alone entered his quiet mind on his drive home. It was a new year — a new beginning for Johnny Apple. And he knew he had Mickey Pond to thank for that.

Mickey left the party soon after playing. Hanna had come up to him after midnight, handed him a check for two hundred dollars, gave him a big hug, and thanked him for playing.

On his drive home Mickey was certain that the older jock with Hanna at the party must have been the same guy she had been "seeing." He had seen them kissing more than once when he was playing. It was obvious to Mickey that she liked the guy; and Mickey was certain that if she had any real love in her heart for Johnny, she would have felt it in his song. That was why he accepted her invitation to play — to find out whether Hanna had real love for Johnny. *How can I tell Johnny this?* he pondered.

It was good for Mickey to return to an empty house. He had been afraid to be alone in the expansive place he had inherited. But all was well.

Late the next afternoon, Johnny paid a visit to Mickey at Prairieville. The two friends had things they wanted to say on the first day of the new year. Mickey had just finished cleaning the oven when Johnny knocked on the front door. There was an easy manner between them when the boy who could fly told Mickey he had been studying for his exam all morning and was feeling confident about it.

"I owe it to you," Johnny smiled. "I was outside Hanna's sorority house last night when you were playing. I couldn't come inside because I was feeling sick about my dad. But by the time you finished playing, I was feeling better than I have felt in a long time."

That's when Mickey told his friend about Hanna's other boyfriend in Mankato, and how he wanted to play at her party just to see if she'd be with him. "She was. She's been dating him since she's been there. It's best you know."

"It doesn't matter. I let her into my head before ... but not anymore. She's part of something that covered up my pain ... the loss of my dad. Hanna's a nice girl, but I'm over her. She can find someone else to fill her time when she comes home."

Mickey bought Johnny dinner at a café in LeRoy, then they went over to Katie's house to let her know what had happened in Mankato. It was in Katie's house that Johnny saw clearly how much Katie cared for him. He assured her he wasn't going to be fooled by Hanna or fool himself anymore.

When Johnny asked Katie where her dad was, she informed him that he was over at Maxine's house. They all had a good laugh when Johnny said, "Just think ... if my mom and Karl get married, we'd all be related."

"Sweet," Mickey smiled.

On the early afternoon of January 4th, Karl, Maxine and the talented trio were all waiting inside the house at Prairieville when Eddie and Lauren arrived in the rental truck with Lauren's car in tow. Johnny had easily passed his exam the day before and had completely broken off his relationship with Hanna. He had called her earlier that morning and told her he didn't want to date her if she was dating someone else.

Lauren and Eddie returned to Prairieville as husband and wife. They had gotten married in Las Vegas and honeymooned on the road, stopping for a day in Lincoln to meet Eddie's family. Eddie told the gathering the news when he carried his bride over the threshold.

Now that Karl and Maxine were seeing more of each other, it was apparent to all of them that they were one big, happy family who were all determined to love and support one another.

That first night alone in front of the fireplace at Prairieville, Lauren and Eddie shared a bottle of wine and talked about the changes they had noticed in their friends.

"Johnny seemed ... different," Lauren noticed.

"Yes, I think so. He did pass his exam."

"But there was a lightness in his eyes ... don't you think?"

"He did seem more alive and happy, now that you mention it. And Karl and Maxine seem to be hitting it off well," Eddie mentioned.

"Yes! Maxine told me she really likes him and respects the way he's been a good father to Katie. And Mickey was so proud of the job you two did on the floors."

"I was proud of him for the hard work he did. He's really come a long way from how he described himself when he was living on that farm in Madisonville. He's making great progress toward being able to live here alone when it's time for us to move on. In the kitchen tonight, Mickey asked me if we were going to have kids. I told him we didn't have any plans to raise children of our own ... that having kids wasn't important to us right now. And he said he feels the same way ... unless he meets someone special like Lauren."

"Aw ... that's so sweet."

"I told him to let me know when he wanted the house to himself. We would be flexible and willing to get our own place whenever he was ready."

"What did he say?"

"He said he liked us living here but didn't want us to feel obligated to stay here. He told me he wanted me to tell him if we wanted to leave and that he would be happy either way ... as long as we lived close by."

"Do you think we'd live close by if we moved?"

"We won't know until we get there," he said as he kissed her forehead.

"Sweet," she grinned.

*Michael is currently living in
Asheville, NC*

mfrederick310@aol.com

Feedback to author:
Michael Frederick
14435 S. 48th St./Apt. 1138
Phoenix, AZ 85044